| AUTHOR | CLASS |
| --- | --- |
| COFFMAN, V | F |

**TITLE** Enemy of love

# Enemy of
# Love

# Enemy of Love

*Virginia Coffman*

PIATKUS

03589505

This edition first published in
Great Britain in 1989 by
Judy Piatkus (Publishers) Ltd of
5 Windmill Street, London W1

British Library Cataloguing in Publication Data

Coffman, Virginia, *1914* –
  Enemy of love.
  I. Title
  813.′54 [F]

  ISBN 0−86188−819−7

Printed and bound in Great Britain by
Billing & Sons Ltd, Worcester

# 1

All too soon that afternoon the lamplighter began to make his rounds of the little London square outside my windows, bringing the night with him. I had come to dread the darkness and any odd, unexpected sounds during the last few days, since I cut myself off from any further contact with Luc Monceau, the French spymaster in London. I was now aware that in this show of defiance against the enemy agent who had employed me, and my parents before me, I had most likely signed my own death warrant.

· Surely it was an ironic situation, to have placed myself in such danger; in a lifetime of twenty-four years I had never thought of England as my country. With an Irish father and a French mother I had very early found my life and politics governed by their ancient hatreds. Until this spring of 1805.

My parents had not lived to see their dreams for Britain's defeat so nearly come to pass. All of Europe had fallen under the influence of French Revolutionary democracy. Only Britain, the aristocratic anachronism, refused to make peace. And here was I, finding myself in sympathy with Britain, that ancient enemy of my parents, at Britain's darkest moment.

My housekeeper, Mrs. Hobbs, had abruptly given her notice that morning, and although she drank heavily and her previous experience was dubious, the loss of her companionship was a blow to me. My parents' work and mine had cut us off from real friendships with other Londoners, and indeed, from other human beings. I took pride in my independence, which shocked those who knew that I lived alone except for the housekeeper-cook, but there was the other side of the coin, the loneliness that such independence entailed.

What endless creakings there were in an old house after dark! Especially when one was alone. I heard a noise like a subdued *click*—a latch raised?—and I went through the tiny reception hall to the front door. Angry at my own fearfulness, I threw the door open in a foolhardy and even dangerous gesture. But there was nothing on the front steps except the faint glow from the nearest lamp in the square. The lamplighter had moved on.

I stepped back inside and bolted the door. I lingered there a minute or two, wondering what sound had disturbed me. What was its source?

Then I remembered Father's pistol. I crossed the hall and went into his study, which I used only when I settled the monthly accounts or dealt with other business of that nature. Although Mrs. Hobbs and I cleaned and dusted the room regularly, it still held the faint scent of Father's particularly revolting pipe tobacco. But the scent was more than welcome now as a reminder of his courage, which I badly needed. From my ring of household keys, I unlocked the small, inlaid desk, reached into the familiar center drawer, and with fingers that shook a little, I felt for Father's loaded pistol. My groping fingers did not immediately locate the silver-inlaid pistol butt, and I stooped to examine the drawer. The pistol was gone.

It had certainly been there last night. I had made quite certain of that, after Mrs. Hobbs mentioned that two females alone needed protection. She saw me bring out the pistol and check it to see that it was properly loaded. She had even made some remark about it, saying what a lucky circumstance that my papa had taught me to use it. . . . I *did* know how to use it? she asked me twice.

And now Mrs. Hobbs was gone very suddenly, giving me only an hour's notice, and Father's pistol was doubtless gone with her. What a fool I had been! Trusting and careless, after all my training. She had probably been given her marching orders by Luc Monceau, who would not want her here to witness and testify to whatever happened to me.

This was all conjecture. I did not know precisely the reason for my housekeeper's sudden departure. But I had counted upon her presence in the house at least until my cousin George arrived. For the first time in his life my soldier cousin claimed to have an idea. His plan was absurd, a proposed marriage between me and George's colonel, a man I had never met. But a meeting with this wife-hunting colonel would at least remove me from London and the revenge of the French agents who, despite my assurances, must fear I would betray their entire organization in England. As if I could betray them without going to the gallows myself! But Luc Monceau never took chances.

I had been haunted in these years since my father's death by the small, infrequent tasks I had been asked to perform just as Father had always performed them. The difference between us was Father's passionate belief in the treason he committed through his dinners with Admiralty friends, his visits with War Office comrades, the bits of gossip he retailed to his employer, Luc Monceau. Monceau appeared to London society as only one of the endless procession of French émigrés who had escaped the horrors of the Revolution. He was living on his personal charm, his wit and the properties inherited from an English grandmother. Only a very few of us knew the deadly truth about his real occupation—the chief of French spies in London.

Years ago, reflecting my parents' belief, I had considered Luc Monceau a hero. I was proud when Father relayed to him such things as a slightly tipsy admiral's boast that England would never give up the Island of Malta, in spite of her government's agreement to do so in the Treaty of Amiens, signed in 1802. It seemed to me admirable to betray such perfidy in England's dealings with France. But after Father's death from dropsy, when I was asked to provide similar bits and pieces of Admiralty and War Office gossip collected from English guests who trusted me, I came to understand Monceau's terrible power. Two people whom I had known, an elderly Englishman and a young French girl, an émigrée, were destroyed, the girl in a street accident involving a runaway coach and team, and the old man by "suicide" with a dueling pistol found in what I knew to be the wrong hand. The two unfortunates had shared one thing: both had told me that they wanted to leave Monceau's employ.

I did not connect the two deaths in my mind until after I myself refused Monceau's last assignment. It involved another betrayal of War Office gossip among officers and their wives at a dinner I attended. Through the indiscretion of a general's loud-spoken lady, I learned that the English were supplying weapons to the black rebels fighting their French rulers on the island of Haiti. I said nothing of this to Monceau, but another of his spies was evidently present at the dinner, because Luc questioned my silence on a matter so vital to France and I asked him to relieve me of future assignments. I explained that I had long felt unnerved, hounded by fears and nightmares, and was sure I would fail him—just such excuses as I thought he might accept. I did not tell him the truth, that I had come to loathe the deceptions I practiced against England.

Luc had merely smiled, that smile which had chilled others of his agents who failed to satisfy him.

Two days later I was nearly run down by a coach and team galloping full tilt through the square outside my own doorstep. A coach with no coachman. Exactly the way the émigrée French girl had died.

After that, I knew.

I could see now, through the partially open portières, that the lamps were all lighted, but they merely provided a flickering contrast to the many dark shadows in and about the square. I snuffed the candles in the little music room and looked out between the portières. Just then a carriage rattled around the park in the center of the square and drew up before the residence occupied by the retired admiral. The coachman dropped down to walk his team, apparently expecting a long wait. I devoutly hoped so. The lanky boy who acted as his postilion trotted over the cobblestones and examined a coach wheel. At least there were two human beings within the sound of my voice.

Absurd to think that I might need the help of two strangers, one of them little more than a child! But fear was taking hold of me. My knowledge of the Emperor Napoleon's premier agent in England was worse than awkward; it was disastrous. Yet one word from me to the authorities would hang me as well as Monceau, and I was not quite that heroic!

In my sudden need for company I found it maddening to see the old admiral and his daughter rustle out of the house across the square much more rapidly than usual. They stepped up into the coach, and in all too short a time my hoped-for assistance was on its way to Carlton House and a ball presided over by the Prince of Wales and his lady, Mrs. Fitzherbert.

The little square remained empty for the next few minutes. I turned away from the long windows, aware that though the spring night was not excessively cold, my skin beneath the muslin gown was chilled through. Earlier I had laid a fire which crackled pleasantly in the sitting room beyond the central staircase. Beckoned by the warmth of the room, I went in. How often this comfortable study had been the scene of meetings between Father and the French agents who pretended to be émigrés and actually lived on British charity!

I held my hands out to the blaze, wondering how long ago I had first sensed the vile duplicity of my family, including myself, as we lived under the protection of a country we betrayed without a qualm. Far too late, with both my parents dead, I had finally hesitated and then, at last, refused to accept the role I had inherited.

From the kettle on the hob I made tea, grateful that Mama had taught me to cook, to care for my clothing, and to conduct household affairs. Even while I employed Mrs. Hobbs, I was not at all certain that I could afford an experienced cook and housemaid on the small quarterly allowance I received from Mama's estate. Father's will plainly demonstrated his low opinion of females by the proviso that Mama's not inconsiderable inheritance would come to me only upon the date of my marriage. The inference was obvious: any gentleman whom I might marry would better care for my money and properties than I myself. That was not necessarily true, but my opinion counted for very little in the matter. I put the teacup to my lips, sighed at the first real comfort I had known in several hours, and again heard a sound somewhere inside the house, a kind of thumping noise. So anxious was I that I held Mama's delicate Limoges cup suspended in midair as I listened. If I called out, my intruder would be warned off and simply return at another time—if he were not provoked to murder me at once. At any other time I might have suspected the noise came from rats in the basement storerooms or from the kitchen, which was also below the street level. But, I thought with grim humor, rats could scarcely cause the kitchen stairs to creak, or that odd thumping noise, as of a body falling, or a man jumping and landing upon his feet. That sound betrayed a human body. One of Luc Monceau's assassins?

At last I set the cup down. I moved from the sitting room to the central staircase, and then to the door behind it which opened onto the basement steps that plunged downward to intense darkness. This door had been left ajar—carefully left ajar, I had no doubt. I closed it with great stealth and shot the bolt. At least whoever was down there had not yet reached the stairs, because I saw no light.

I turned away, my mind whirling with gruesome pictures of weapons I might use—a carving knife from the stillroom on this floor, one of those very useful pokers by the hearth in the sitting room. Even a club of broomstraws stored in the pantry beyond the stillroom. And that put me in mind of the heavy pantry door opening onto the stable walk behind these houses on the east side of the square. The lamp on the newel post of the front stairs cast a faded, slightly flickering glow that served to show me the way through the ground-floor stillroom and then the pantry. The outside door appeared to be securely locked. But did Mrs. Hobbs have a key? At all events, I shot the bolt as a double precaution and started back toward the front of the house.

As I stepped into the narrow passage in front of the basement stairs, I saw the latch of the basement door turn slowly, then more rapidly, as if touched by the beginnings of panic. If I ran, if I screamed, I would save myself momentarily, but I might never know the identity of the prowler, and the attempt could be repeated at any time. I ran back into the pantry, found the broom, and carefully hefted it with its sharp, curving straws like a club over my head. With my other hand I slipped the bolt free again, hoping that the intruder would believe the door of the basement stairs had merely stuck the first time the latch was tried.

My heart had slowed its beat, my hand felt frozen to the broom handle. But I was ready. I watched the door pulled open, raised the broom again, and brought it down· furiously to within a hair's breadth of the intruder before I saw that he was a child, a very grimy, surprised boy of about eight. His torn breeches smelled of soot, his bare legs and hands bore the scars of old· burns. A chimney sweep's boy, obviously. I dropped the broom with a clatter and took the boy's arm, but as he winced, I let him go. Before he could use his wits to escape, I asked him sternly, "Who sent you here at this hour?"

His lively eyes regarded me with such innocence that I wanted to shake him, but did not.

"Me, mum? Sent, mum? I lost meself an' now they'll be searchin' me out, surely."

I tried not to be deterred by his all-too-familiar and

likable brogue. "Never you mind. Tell me now. Was it a foreign gentleman?"

"Foreign? No, mum. No frog as went and give me no orders." Innocence fairly shone from that knowing young face.

"Then how do you know it was a frog? I mean, a Frenchman?"

He bit his tongue, then flashed an ingratiating grin.

"Did I say that now? A slip it was. I seen no frog— no Frenchie, what I mean to say. Not for ever so."

# 2

I beckoned him out of the doorway and asked if anyone else was down there in the dark. Then, assured by his genuine surprise that he was alone, I bolted the basement door and shoved him gently into the study. He delighted in the fire. While he put his work-blackened hands to the flames and then turned and exposed the backside of his tattered breeches to the heat, sighing ecstatically, I observed him. However contemptible my work as a spy had been, it had taught me much about human nature. This little chimney sweep had volunteered to commit some petty act against me, undoubtedly on the promise of more payment than he had ever earned in his wretched profession, but he himself was not about to plunge a knife into my heart, or shoot or poison me. Still . . . he might not be above opening a door from the inside of my house, permitting my real murderer to reach me. Certainly he knew Luc Monceau or one of his agents. That mistake about "the frog," our nasty English slang for the French enemy, was clear enough.

Watching him now, I considered how best to reach him.

"What are you called, boy?"

"Me? Paddy, they calls me. Me Aunt Meg, that is to say."

"You live with your aunt?"

My question had struck a sympathetic chord in him. He stopped warming himself long enough to clasp his burned and sooty hands in a wistful gesture.

"Not but what I'd give a golden guinea to live with me Aunt Meg, if I had a golden guinea. I'm articled to Old Grizzenby what has the chimneys nigh to the frog's lodgings. For tenpence I'm to lay open the stable door, the one by the pantry-like." He repeated with sparkle, "Tenpence it is, mum, just for a-doing of that bit about the door."

So Mrs. Hobbs had no outside doorkey, after all! That was one relief.

I had never stopped to examine a chimney sweep at such close quarters, or to see the scars left by his hideous task. I knew vaguely that these boys were let down inside our chimneys where they made some effort to clean out the debris, but I had no notion that these children were burned and seared, scarred for their short lives. While my parents and I had busied ourselves in trying to betray a royalist government, we had made no effort to understand, much less alleviate, the conditions of children in our immediate quarter of London. Like so many other visionaries, we had never practiced our dreams at home. At the moment, however, I was in no position to practice anything but self-preservation, and, I hoped, some small charity toward this boy.

"The Frenchie asked you to unbolt the door opening onto the stable yard?"

"Aye, mum. Naught else. For tenpence."

"But if *you* got into my house, why was there a need for you to open the door for another?"

He grinned. "A-cause they wasn't fit to squeeze in the kitchen window like me."

I could believe that. The kitchen, being below the level of the square, had two tiny windows near its ceiling. The windows opened onto the wrought-iron fence separating my house and others from the square. The boy was right. None but a child could have wriggled into that kitchen window. Even then, he must have dropped down a considerable distance to the kitchen's hard stone floor.

"When is the other man coming?"

Paddy shrugged. "Sure, it's only a little robbery. And you—a lady what's such a toff!"

"*When?*"

He jumped and ducked away as if he expected to be struck. I added hastily, "All right, Paddy. I wouldn't hurt you. But I must know."

The boy recovered his equilibrium rapidly, flashing all his teeth in that contagious grin of his.

"The frog, he cuffed me one when I hid and made like I'd hear 'em talking. They give me a toss. But I know, all the same. It's to be midnight, or as near as makes no matter."

"And he is to enter by the pantry door in the stable yard?"

"Aye, mum. Would you be saying now that I did you a mite of good, mum? That's to say, would it be worth sixpence, say?"

It was my turn to smile. "It very well might be. Now, Paddy, I want you to leave this area, leave the man who employs you, and go to your Aunt Meg. Where is she?"

"Off to Rye, or nigh onto it. But, mum, you'd never send me there. Why, it'll be that dear you've no notion."

I knew that Rye was a village southwest of London, in Sussex, with a rather unsavory reputation for smuggling and the resultant murders of excisemen trying to collect His Majesty's revenues. However, Paddy showed every sign of being able to tread warily in a dangerous world.

"You must never again see this Frenchie," I said. "He will know you have helped me and he will have you killed and your body thrown into some alley. Do you understand?"

He was wise beyond his years. His eyes widened briefly before they narrowed in thought. He glanced over his shoulder into the darkness behind the main staircase.

"You'll be saying, mum, it was for to do you ill that the frog made me open the stable-yard door."

"Precisely. He wants to murder me."

"But you'll send for the Bow Street Runners to catch the frog?"

I couldn't explain that it was impossible to turn Luc Monceau over to a thief-catching group like the Bow Street organization. And if I were able to kill Monceau's hired assassin, perhaps with the aid of my cousin George Adare, there would be the awkwardness of the body to explain. Not to mention the revolting business of murder itself.

"Paddy, I want you to take the Hastings coach to-night, and make your way to your Aunt Meg."

"Dover Mail's hard by my Aunt Meg's coteen. I like the Dover Mail."

"Yes, yes. Anything. But you must never mention the frog—I mean, the Frenchman. If you do, he will come and find you and kill you. And your Aunt Meg."

Bless the boy! I could see that the mention of his Aunt Meg's danger influenced his decision.

"I'll do it, mum. I'll even book on Hastings coach. I know how the thing is done."

"Good." I went to my father's desk and found the locked box where Father had kept his cash, which I used for unexpected expenses. Fortunately, Mrs. Hobbs had not taken the cash box. Perhaps she had considered this would be too obvious and would count against her if I actually did make hire of the Bow Street Runners to track her down. I was not afraid of what my mischievous young friend might think if he saw this money. I would not be remaining here after tonight in any case. I would not dare to remain after what I devoutly hoped would be the failure of Monceau's assassin.

"You mentioned a golden guinea," I said, removing the entire gold and silver contents of the box. "Would you carry a golden guinea to your Aunt Meg? She must have money to care for you. You have promised me you will not return to your chimney-sweep master."

"Aye, mum, but—" For the first time he seemed at a loss. He looked at the money, then his sooty eyebrows wrinkled with the effort to think through his problem. As for me, while he mumbled that "golden guineas was the best, but—" my attention shifted to the danger that must be approaching this house all too rapidly. I listened to the usual creaking of the old house, and scooping the money into my reticule, I hurried out of the study to the back passage. All doors were locked and bolted. From the minuscule pantry window I could see the moonlit stable yard. Nothing out there but a cat, prowling for a warm place to curl up and sleep. I envied him. I too would like to know I could sleep tonight in comfort and safety.

When I returned I was startled to bump into the

boy. He had been following me into the half-dark of the hall.

"There's a fine big toff out in the square, mum."

Nervously, I set him aside and rushed to look out the music-room window. I had been afraid I would see one of Monceau's murderous friends, but even at this distance from the south end of the square, I could not mistake my good-natured cousin George. He fairly sparkled in his regimentals as he stuck his head and shoulders from a huge, rumbling old coach, to give orders to the driver. This old-fashioned carriage was apparently to aid him in rescuing me from "a troublesome suitor," for that was the explanation I had given for the necessity of a hasty escape. Father had early taught me not to reveal any of our work to Cousin George. "Silly popinjay!" was his designation for my long, lanky cousin, but perhaps Father was unfair, for George had always been good-hearted and from our earliest childhood had obeyed me in everything.

I relieved Paddy's nervousness by assuring him that the fine gentleman was a friend. I added quickly, "Can you slip across town to the booking office for the Dover Mail without letting anyone see you?"

"Like I was a shadow, mum. Only—if you'll be that kind—it's best not gold, mum. Nobody'd believe it of Aunt Meg. Nor me. Best it's plain silver. Or copper. Aye. Copper."

A very bright boy. Nevertheless, when I emptied coppers and silver into his palms, he stammered, "F-for me? You'll give it to me for k-keeps?"

"For Aunt Meg to keep for you. Now, be careful. Shall I ask Captain Adare to escort you to the end of the square?"

"Beggin' your pardon, I best go as I come. None of them frogs can get in that way."

I heard George clanking up the front steps but I went with Paddy to the basement door, opening it to give the child some illumination. Meanwhile he was dropping coins into half a dozen unsuspected hiding places in his tattered jerkin and breeches. As he reached the bottom step he looked up, his teeth bright in the darkness.

"You can throw the bolt on the door now, mum. There's light from the square down here." He thanked me and reminded me again to throw the bolt. My cousin was banging at the front door, so I did as Paddy asked, but before I returned to the front of the house I looked out at the stable yard again. It occurred to me that if I wanted to protect Paddy I had best leave the pantry door unbolted, in order to throw Monceau's man off the scent of Paddy's trickery. I did so, then went to welcome George Adare.

My cousin and I embraced. I was not usually nervous with men. I had known, and even ruled a few in my twenty-four years, and never until now had I been literally dependent upon a man. Cousin George was neither strong-bodied nor quick-minded enough for this post, but I must count upon the poor man. He could use my money, and I must have his help in getting out of London. I did wonder, though, how I could take advantage of George's offer to help me without flatly agreeing to marry his colonel in some far-off Caribbean stronghold. I found that Cousin George was his frank—too frank—self.

"Not looking your best, old girl. And that won't do. Won't do at all. I've counted on those green eyes of yours, and that fair hair. He sees too many brunettes on St. Sebastien, if you take my meaning. 'She's a modern female,' I said to Ian, 'but not one of that Wollstonecraft woman's horrors.' That would be too modern by half. You've lost more weight as well, cuz. Worrying over that pesky suitor, I daresay." He evidently believed my story about escaping an unwanted suitor. "Well, we'll relieve you of all that. But I expressly told you to gain a trifling amount. Ian's women are usually females with some meat on their bones."

A pretty prospect, I could see! Here was what I had dreaded, the assumption that I must marry his superior, Ian Douglas. Surely there ought to be a place for a decent, unmarried female on the Caribbean island of St. Sebastien where Cousin George hoped to make his fortune. And I had heard often enough of Colonel Ian Douglas's detestation of women except in the sexual line, a loathing based upon an early experience of matrimony and, doubtless, upon a complete ignorance of how to make a woman happy. I found such creatures challenging but hardly endearing. They aroused in me all my battling instincts.

But Colonel Douglas, Governor of St. Sebastien, would have very little interest in a woman who had been trained in the proud, self-confident, and free style of the late female rights exponent, Mrs. Wollstonecraft. I was rather more tall than the average woman, and capped this initial disadvantage by having pale-blond hair and easily sunburned features rather than the rich brown hair and olive complexion made all the vogue by some of the Prince of Wales's ladies. We were living in an age when our poor King George, mentally ill, had very little to say about his own kingdom, and his eldest son ruled us all with, I sometimes thought, more attention to the color of his mistress's hair than the condition of his subjects.

But my first object was to escape the long arm of Luc Monceau. "We must hurry," I reminded Cousin

George. "I have my portmanteau and several band-boxes, if you will be so kind."

"Gad's life, cuz! I'd no notion your unwanted suitors were so persistent. You act as though your life itself were at stake." But with his long stride he soon covered the distance to the bedchamber on the first floor where with grunts and groans, he picked up my baggage. I, meanwhile, looked about me at all the possessions I might be leaving for a great while, perhaps never to see again. Furnishings chosen by Mama long ago. Lovely things, but representing a life that had become deadly for me.

I flung my best green silk-lined cloak around my shoulders, drawing the hood well over my face while I took my portmanteau from my complaining cousin and prayed that Monceau's man would not see me as we left the house.

Outside the quiet, sedate-looking house, so like the others in the square, I rushed to the carriage and climbed in. After disposing of my boxes, George joined me, giving the coachman the signal to start. The team leaped forward and George fell across me, all arms and legs and glitter in his bright scarlet tunic. This minor disaster made us both laugh, and breaking the somber mood that had been entirely of my own making. Cousin George could always be counted upon for a cheerful disposition, a quality that—quite unfairly—sometimes set my teeth on edge.

"Well, old girl," he began. I was some sixteen months older than Cousin George and he never forgot it. "If you must flee the city to escape unwelcome suitors, I've found a very safe means of cutting away the fellow's attention, if you will only listen to my plan. Though damn, I do much prefer administering a touch of the fine old home-brewed to the fellow." He doubled a fist and demonstrated by a fierce jab at the worn velvet cushions behind us.

"No, no! Think of the scandal!"

He looked his surprise, as well he might. No court had seen more scandal recently than that of our poor king's all too lively son. But even more significant, George knew I had seldom acted coy. My method of handling various suitors had been to laugh, to tease in a friendly manner, to commit myself no further than to a light flirtation. If that failed, I became direct and matter-of-fact.

I tried not to let George observe my nervousness while I glanced out the windows. We were leaving the square, and I thought I made out a figure in a dark traveling coat and bicorne hat moving stealthily behind the houses on its eastern side. The man was headed toward the stable yard. But he could have been anyone. And it still lacked an hour until midnight.

George reminded me in a hurt voice, "You haven't asked me more about my scheme with old Ian for your rescue. Have you no interest in your future? It's all settled, you know."

I had been terribly remiss there. I owed so much to George, probably even my life. I reached for his hand and squeezed it. My own fingers were so chilled that they must have startled him, but he seemed pleased. He swallowed hard, and watched me with a certain anxiety.

"Georgie dear, I am sorry. I was so worried, I forgot to thank you." It was utterly absurd that anyone should imagine his colonel and I, two mature persons, would marry without at least a reasonable acquaintance. To confess the truth, I was much too independent of spirit to consider such a degrading and primitive method of acquiring a master. But it amused me to talk of it.

"Tell me more about this crabbed commander who hates females but demands a wife he has never laid eyes upon."

"Saw your miniature, old girl. The one I used to carry."

"And he lays his happiness in the hands of a woman in a picture?" More likely, he knew that if he married me, he would gain control of my inheritance.

"Quite a good likeness. He won't do much better than my cousin Madeline. And so I told him."

I moistened my dry, stiff lips. I felt a curious mingling of revulsion and excitement. From what I had heard of Colonel Ian Douglas I pictured a martinet, a harsh soldier who cared more about the native and French population he ruled than about his English superiors, and certainly more than he would ever care about a wife. But it would be an exciting challenge to master and enjoy the love of such a man!

"Can you be serious? Colonel Douglas knows nothing of me, nothing of my habits, my manners . . ."

"Rubbish. I've discussed you with him many a time, and of course, he was interested enough in your miniature to keep it. Or possibly he just forgot to return it. Hard to say, with Ian. But he knows all, even your independent habits. And your age, naturally."

"My age!" I bristled. "And how old is this paragon?"

"Late thirties, I expect. Ideal age. For you, that is to say."

For a second or two I wanted to hit him, but I knew I was being unfair. The world must feel very much as Cousin George did in regard to the respective ages of males and females. I tried to control my anger through a consideration of the advantages of escaping Luc Monceau. It was almost worth marrying a stranger in order to be free of him.

"I imagine I might take a ship for St. Sebastien and meet your colonel. Then, if we should find each other . . . compatible—well, who knows?"

I was positive we would never find each other in the least compatible. Colonel Douglas hated females, while I detested such prejudiced men. The power and strength of the man intrigued me because it was said that he used that power for the good of his silly little island which the British Navy had captured in this eternal war with France, but at the same time I could not forget that his tiny Caribbean "kingdom" had been stolen from France, which my parents had loved and worked for throughout their lives.

George disagreed at once, however. "Won't do at all, cuz. Old Ian needs a wife and no mistake. For the socializing. Needs a female—a lady—to unite the Frenchies and the free blacks with us British. All friends. Good citizens. You know the sort of thing."

I began to understand. Perhaps Colonel Douglas thought an unknown woman would serve as well as any other for such purely practical and social purposes. It wasn't as though an arranged marriage between strangers was uncommon. In my mother's country and even here in England such marriages were quite the thing. But not, I thought, for a woman of twenty-four who had lived with merely a housekeeper to give her countenance. I was much too used to having my own way in life.

In spite of my age, which Cousin George so ungallantly stressed, I suppose I must have dreamed of quite a different marriage. I wanted to love my husband as my mother had my father, with a great, all-encompassing love. But crude, female-hating Colonel Douglas was not a man with whom I felt I could share anything except, possibly, a desire to improve the relations between the heterogeneous people of St. Sebastien. Yes, that *was* something we could share, after all. And if this Colonel Douglas were amenable to the influence of a wife . . . who could say? It might be an acceptable marriage.

"Come, old girl. I promised to escort you to Plymouth, and by gad, I shall. What with changes, fresh teams, meals, et cetera, I may even have time to persuade you that the colonel's offer is—well, unexceptionable." I smiled and he hurried on, "A beautiful female alone needs a protector. I've always maintained that."

"Thank you, George. I would have to be in dire straits before I should consider marrying a brute who genuinely detested women. Of course, if his hostility is based upon one bad experience, one might forgive . . . . But it is very good of you to take me out of London."

"You see?" he said in triumph. "You needed a man tonight, to rescue you. Though, frankly, I wish I might give a severe dressing-down to this suitor of yours who causes you to flee from your native haunts, as it were." I smiled at the formality of his speech, gained from an early education by his mama, who read an excessive number of novels. "Well, then, we'll forget your unwelcome suitor and think about the more welcome one. I have reasons for suggesting this flight to Plymouth. You see, I sail from Plymouth in three days' time. Bound for the Caribbean and St. Sebastien."

I stared at him. "George! You rogue! You intend

that I shall not have time to think. Am I to go with you at once?"

"Why not? My business with the War Office is completed. I have persuaded them we need some of the new issue of weapons, and I did promise the colonel I would bring you with me. One doesn't say no to old Ian."

"Doesn't one?" My chin went up at this challenge. "Perhaps I would be a good influence on old Ian, after all is said."

He grinned. I began to wonder if my simple cousin was not deliberately goading me into something I would bitterly regret.

# 3.

The myriad colors in the Caribbean were breathtaking after the gloomy gray of the Atlantic. But much more important to those of us aboard the little barque *Maud Vester* were the calm waters after weeks of such seasickness that I had regretted Luc Monceau's failure to kill me.

I had very nearly let George Adare sail without me. I knew in Plymouth that if I set foot on that small ship bobbing at anchor, my life and my not inconsiderable properties would thereafter belong to a stranger, and an unpleasant stranger at that. To be bound for life to a man like Colonel Douglas might be like existing in a prison cell. No, worse than a cell, for I would not even possess the freedom of my own body.

Yet three days of persuasion by my cousin, as well as the arrival of a sinister French émigré at the Plymouth Arms Inn, began to place Colonel Douglas's offer in a better light. I must have read the colonel's letter of proposal a score of times before I could find anything to recommend the man:

*"Madam: Captain Adare will have presented my proposal to you and its purpose. I do not offer the usual pap of eternal devotion. I honor your intelligence too much to imagine you would be swayed by such protes-*

*tations. The age at which you have arrived unwed tells me that you are keenly aware of the pitfalls of the ordinary marriage.*

*"Should you desire to assist me in my present task, in which your role would be social and educational, then I may promise you my protection and a certain standing as the first lady of this exotically beautiful, though uncalm island.*

*"I have the honor to sign myself your hopeful suitor, Ian McClellan Douglas."*

What an impossible man! No charm whatever. With the head and hands of a crabbed old bull, I had no doubt. Yet . . . wasn't there a wistful note in that letter? A need and dependence upon me? I wondered what my "hopeful suitor" meant by an "uncalm island," but George swept this aside.

"A matter of local rebels. Nothing serious. You must remember these native people are fighting the French in Haiti, and they would like nothing better than to add the English to their conquests. But old Ian seems to have taken steps toward peace with their leader, a native called Le Maréchal. If you remain in the town of Port Fleur or at Government House on the promontory above the port, all should be serene. They don't usually make their forays into town."

Not too encouraging, but if I wanted excitement, it was obvious I should find it on that tropical island which, I had been assured by my future husband, was exotically beautiful. It seemed a fascinating challenge to me, even if it did prove as dangerous as my former employer, Luc Monceau.

On that last night before Cousin George and I sailed on the *Maud Vester,* it seemed to me that the sinister French newcomer to the inn followed me everywhere.

I could not escape him, although I saw to it that I was never entirely alone. But George had to board the ship before the regular passengers, and I wondered if anything could be worse than, from that moment, to live in terror of every stranger with a French accent in England. Someday I would fail to avoid one particular stranger, and afterward Luc Monceau would sleep again, knowing I could not betray his identity.

So in the end I revised my fears and my revulsion toward marriage to an unpleasant stranger, assuring myself that if we found ourselves incompatible at first meeting, or during the days before the ceremony, when we would become acquainted, we might part amicably with no harm done. And there were other considerations. I did not suppose Ian Douglas would make many physical demands upon me, since, if George was right, the man had become a hopeless womanhater and would avoid me except as I was socially useful to him.

All these arguments, however, seemed less than convincing on that bright crystal morning when George and I stood leaning over the taffrail at the stern of the ship and studied first our wake, white and foaming against the aquamarine waters around us, and then, moving around to the larboard side, caught our first glimpse of the raw, forbidding green world that loomed up before us.

"There she rises. Your future kingdom, cuz," George remarked happily.

"It is exceedingly . . . green, isn't it?" I ventured. I had never seen a landscape so rich, soil so dark, or mountain slopes that depth of green that was almost black.

"Jungles." George dismissed it all with an airy wave. "A lively place if you've an interest in wild flora and fauna. Myself, I don't venture off the beaten path, I can tell you. There are creatures in that jungle that whites have never seen before. Ever seen an alligator?"

"No! Nor care to, unless I am well protected."

"Stay away from the jungles, that's all there is to it. The fer-de-lance, for instance. There's an ugly customer. Deadly poison. A serpent, you know. But you aren't likely to see one. Quite pretty, old Ian says. But he's a taste for oddities anyway."

Oddities including a wife he had never seen. But I did not express my thought aloud. Having come this far, I was determined to make the best of a distasteful bargain.

"Bit of a fuss getting all the cargo off," George said. "And a nice snug little nest of rifles I'm delegated to deliver to the colonel. I'll leave you now. They'll likely be putting you and the other passengers ashore before the cargo. Sure you can manage without me?"

"Quite sure, dear George. You've been an amazing comfort to me." I hoped he did not guess how nervous I was at my immediate prospect, a meeting with the man to whom I might give my entire life.

We embraced and he went his way, his long legs devouring deck space as he proceeded up toward the bow and then, as if by magic, disappeared to wherever the colonel's precious rifles were stored. I stared at the rapidly approaching harbor and surrounding promontories of Port des Fleurs—Port Fleur, as George had called it in the English style. Not for nothing had the little town been given its name. Even at this distance and without the spyglass which the captain used with such intense concentration, I could see enormous tropical flowers, purple hedges, walls of red blooms—a perfect disguise for the wretched taverns, coopers' shops, and assorted other clapboard shacks that bordered the semicircular curve of the waterfront street.

The *Maud Vester*'s tough, evil-looking Captain Hollin, whose disposition was soft as whey, startled me as he put down his spyglass and spoke almost at my shoulder.

"Good morning, miss. You've in love with it already? It's the usual thing, they say."

"Good morning, sir . . . who are *they?*"

"Them that visited Port Fleur when the island was owned by the Frenchies. Not so popular now, what with the change of government and the rebellion, and that."

I glanced from the town with its dusty little *savane,* the grassy patch in the center of the semicircle, to what must be Government House, a beautiful white Palladian front building. Fortresslike, it was set high upon the south promontory of the harbor, at a level considerably above the town. It would be much cooler there, I decided with relief. I was so used to the damp northern climate of London that I found the humid heat here on deck to be suffocating, and I suspected it must be much worse in the town.

I fanned my flushed face with the charming and highly practical folding paper fan presented to me by Captain Hollin. Studying its careful workmanship, I thanked him again for the gift.

"I have a notion I shall find your gift exceedingly valuable, sir. You are an artist."

He grinned, but a warm flush of embarrassment softened his features amazingly. "Well, now!" And after an instant's thought, he repeated, "Well, now!"

I glanced once more at the small fortress on the promontory, cleared my throat, and asked him, "Are you acquainted with the new British governor?"

"Douglas, eh? Good soldier. Brusque fellow with a tongue like a fer-de-lance. But you'll blunt the sharpness. A lovely lady like yourself. Aye, that's all he needs. Same as me. My sweet Sarah made a new man of me, that she did."

"Where does Mrs. Hollin live?" I asked curiously, wondering at a marriage that survived upon visits of a few weeks a year.

"Falmouth, that's where my Sarah has her bunk. Oh, here we are. A chair for you, miss, and the other . . . er, ladies aboard."

The other ladies were three extraordinary-looking females who had enlivened the long voyage with their good humor and easy acceptance of the tribulations that had befallen us. Even during their bouts of seasickness they were grateful for any attention to them, and afterward, when I too became deathly sick, they paid me in kind. Agnes Mabberly, the pert redhead, led her cohorts up the companionway into the waist of the ship and over to the rail. The *Maud Vester* had dropped anchor now, and all the noise, the running feet, and bellowing voices told me we were about to be deposited on that lush little dot among the leeward isles of the Caribbean.

"Come, Miss Adare," the captain called to me. "Courage, now. You're quite safe."

I thanked him again as I sat down in the absurd but handy contrivance, the canvas-seated chair about to be lowered over the side by pulleys, into the longboat. Holding to the ropes with one gloved hand, I waved to Agnes Mabberly and her girls. The buxom beauties blew airy kisses to me, and Agnes added, "You've our good wishes, miss. About the ogre, you know," and she winked. The ogre was the girls' code word for Colonel Ian Douglas. With one last wave, I felt myself descending rapidly, passing the black-and-white hull of the little ship, and being deposited with bone-shattering suddenness in the longboat.

George helped me from the chair, but he was clearly more anxious to oversee the loading of his colonel's precious rifles. He looked far up the hull of the barque and over our heads, ignoring the ascent of the canvas sling chair.

Now Agnes Mabberly had seated herself and began to be lowered. Two sailors in the longboat who were delegated to help George with his rifles now rushed past me to assist Agnes who, with her girls, had been friendly to them on the long voyage. I saw that Agnes was swinging hard against the hull and had put her hand to her mouth, clearly feeling an attack of nausea. I reached up my handkerchief to her and she clutched it as a drowning man clutches a floating spar. Almost at the same time I saw a wooden box swinging overhead, a box roughly the size and shape of a coffin.

George was shouting, "Wait, damn you! Wait till the ladies are down."

Agnes and one of her girls screamed. I called anxiously to George, "Tell them not to lower the box yet!" I pressed tight against the ship's hull, feeling the sticky pitch and oil and water seep into my coat and best sprigged muslin gown. In the confusion of those seconds, with everyone screaming at cross-purposes, the coffin began to slip through its confining ropes. George and the sailors leaped toward us women. The coffin tilted again, slipped out of the ropes, and crashed across the opposite end of the longboat, spilling rifles over the broken box and into the bright aquamarine waters.

Blinking through the storm of spray and splintered wood, I made out George's long, red-jacketed figure on his knees in the waist of the boat, trying to grab the lost rifles as they sank beyond his reach to the bottom of the harbor.

"George! Are you all right?"

He waved one arm at me, apparently in reassurance. Agnes Mabberly's usually laughing, cheerful countenance appeared strained, as I daresay my own looked. She clutched at my coat sleeve.

"It was an accident, wasn't it?"

"Of course, it was! Why do you—" I did not finish my question. I followed her quick glance upward at the hanging loops of rope, and heard Agnes's breathless murmur, "Missed your cousin by that much! And if you hadn't reached back to give me your handkerchief, it wouldn't have missed you by much more."

I wasn't concentrating upon the import of her words. She was obviously unnerved by the experience as well as by the rapid and dizzying descent in the canvas seat. Besides, the ship's crew was now buzzing around like an angry—or panicked?—swarm, to see if the end of the broken box had done any serious damage to the longboat as it crashed and broke up against an oarlock. Apparently we were safe and could be rowed to the little quai which now swarmed with excited, staring, shouting citizens and slaves of St. Sebastien.

And a colorful crowd it was, too! Nearly as colorful as the many little sailing vessels of assorted sizes, from Mediterranean feluccas with striped sails, to three-masted barkentines that covered the harbor waters. I guessed at the nationalities. There seemed to be few European countries represented, since most of them were associated with the Emperor Napoleon and the French, but one of their allies, a Yankee brig from England's late colonies, lay at anchor across the harbor. Although there were no French ships about, many of the crowd on the quai looked to be in the French mode. I felt a twinge of sadness at France's loss of this exotic little island, but the people seemed in good spirits, and at first glance there was no visible wreckage of war.

Agnes Mabberly, her two girls, and I were to be rowed ashore at once, but George was in a panic, demanding that no one leave the ship's side until the rifles were recovered. He was overruled by the captain of the *Maud Vester* and the bo'sun's mate, a heavy, leather-faced young man who ignored poor George's protests and ordered the sailors to get to their oars. My cousin finally seated himself beside me but kept staring anxiously back into the clear waters at the lost cargo.

"Old Ian will be damned angry!" he muttered to me in explanation. "He counted on those rifles. Couldn't get anything decent out of the War Office, so I bought the rifles myself."

I caught Agnes Mabberly's puzzled gaze, her frown, and was reminded of that curious and horrifying idea she had expressed. I stared up again at the dangling ropes, but more important, at the sailors who had operated the unloading of the box full of rifles. They were scrambling about, hauling up the rope nooses, and as I watched, one of the men startled us by diving overboard, splashing into the water so close to us that we were all badly soaked by the spray.

The sailors at the oars of our boat suddenly shifted their weight forward in unison, and the longboat seemed to leap forward across the harbor. But George was leaning out over the water, shouting orders and offering bribes to the sailor for the rescue of the scattered rifles. I had no notion whether the guns might still be useful after being lodged on the bottom of the bay, but George was either optimistic or desperate. When our boat approached the crowded quai, George gave up shouting instructions to the swimming sailor and to several black island boys who had swum out to help in the recovery. George turned to me. He actually looked pallid with anxiety.

"Old Ian is going to break me for this. He counted on extra weapons. Those damnable guns are going directly to Le Maréchal. Wait and see."

I watched the native boys diving in a circle around the lost rifles, and wondered if George might be right about the destination of the guns. At the same time I found myself stiff with tension which had its roots in fear. Was it fear of some deliberate "accident" that had so nearly befallen me? But it had barely missed George as well. Could it be that Luc Monceau's hand reached so far?

When I considered my icily sweating palms and my reluctance for this longboat's voyage to end, I admitted that something else terrified me as much as the unloading accident. I must soon place myself under the frigid eyes of George's dragon, the man who expected me to marry him. My resolve stiffened. Colonel Douglas would be made to understand that this preposterous wedding must not occur until we had come to know each other. A matter of weeks, at the least. Perhaps months.

Meanwhile, at the end of the quai, a slim young native soldier in a scarlet jacket very similar to my cousin George's uniform, made his way through the chattering throng. He reached out a neat, gloved hand to take the rope hurled at him by George.

"Ahoy, Felipe!" my cousin called out. "Here at last. How've things gone? Quiet, I daresay." He was talking so rapidly, pouring out words, that I wondered if this demonstrated an uneasiness in him as great as my own.

The young officer on the dock, staggeringly handsome, and undoubtedly aware of his attraction for the females surrounding him, took the mooring rope in one hand while saluting with the other.

"*Bonjour, Monsieur le Capitaine!* You are a very long time on your voyage."

"Ran into heavy weather in the Atlantic. Any more trouble with Le Maréchal?"

Agnes's girls, tow-haired Phoebe with her air of innocent abandon, and darker, older María-Vega, stared at Lieutenant Felipe with open admiration. I too had been impressed by his stunning good looks, and was observing him carefully. At George's question about the rebel leader, his eyelids flickered and that sculptured mouth set in a tight line. Then, almost at once, he smiled blandly. I wondered if I might be making preposterous assumptions on little evidence, but when he spoke, I did not believe him.

"Oh, the noble Black Messiah! No, only the usual ambushes. A small trouble at the Boiling Lake. But I believe Colonel Douglas has some notion of a parley. Let us hope his dreams of peace are well founded."

"Just so. Just so." George leaped up to the quai beside him and turned back to help me out of the longboat, which had begun to sweep rhythmically against the quai. "Can you come up, old girl?"

Lieutenant Felipe gave over the mooring line to one of the sailors who had scrambled up on the quai, and then helped my cousin hand me up as well. I thanked him, grateful both for his quick assumption of my identity and for his welcome.

"Mademoiselle Adare, of course. It could be no

other. We on St. Sebastien have long heard that the colonel's lady was the most beautiful woman in London. We can believe that now."

It was impossible not to be warmed into an excellent humor by this effusive flattery.

"You are very generous, Lieutenant, and we are grateful to you for your trouble in meeting us." I tried not to let him guess that I was hurt over the indifference of my future husband, who had not thought "his lady's" arrival worth the short trip down from his fortress to the harbor. But evidently Lieutenant Felipe was skilled in reading what was not said.

When George had belatedly presented the lieutenant to me and was assisting Agnes Mabberly and her girls, the lieutenant began to stroll along the quai beside me.

"I am delegated to express Colonel Douglas's regret that he could not be here to receive you. But the colonel is a very busy man and he makes it a policy that nothing shall interfere with . . . whatever tasks he has undertaken."

I found myself speechless at this remark, and could not guess whether it was the detestable Ian Douglas's conduct or merely Lieutenant Felipe's bitingly frank expression of it that cut me more deeply.

With an enormous effort I managed to lie gracefully. "Such devotion to duty is admirable. As for me, I will appreciate being shown to whatever quarters are provided for me, and perhaps, in the next few days— when it is convenient—we shall meet, the colonel and I, and discuss our possible betrothal."

The lieutenant smiled as though I had said something playfully humorous.

"How delightful to find a lady who can jest at such

a moment! As you are doubtless aware, my pleasant task is to escort you to the Mairie in the town, where the ceremony will take place within the hour."

I must have looked as aghast as I felt.

"Ceremony? What . . . ceremony?"

"Since the Revolution we follow the French style here. If a religious ceremony is desired later, that will be for you and your husband to arrange. But it is the civil marriage service, a very brief one—do not be troubled on that score—which will take place today."

# 4

We were still walking as he spoke, but I couldn't remember taking the steps; it was all distinctly mechanical. I looked back over my shoulder at the *Maud Vester,* wondering when those sails would be unfurled again, when the ship would sail on to its next harbor in these blue-green waters. I no longer recalled the seasick days and nights, the fat salt pork, the gradual disappearance of vegetables, the tiny, foul-smelling cabin. All I could think of was the possibility of escaping from what had suddenly become a nightmare.

"George . . . my cousin," I said desperately, trying to stop, to look around. Anything that would take up time. "I must talk to my cousin. I forgot to tell him about—about—"

"We are approaching the Mairie now, mademoiselle. You see how simple it all is. One of our most useful heritages from the late French Revolution. Even you English may profit by these customs which prevailed here before we were fortunate enough to become an object of interest to the British Navy."

He might now be a loyal subject of King George III, but a residue of his old loyalties to France seemed to remain. I could not dislike him for that. Perhaps I could even trust him with my own doubts and fears.

"Lieutenant, I must tell you, I have no intention of

marrying your colonel without having first become acquainted with him."

"Certainly not, mademoiselle. But introductions will occupy a mere minute or two. Then all may proceed correctly."

Was he being deliberately obtuse?

"You see," he went on brightly, "we have moved upward one square. The town is built upon layers beginning at the waterfront. One day, perhaps we will have built to the top of those cliffs behind the town. We have great plans. Great hopes. That modest building at the head of this street is the home of all our civil affairs, except the judicial and the legislative. Naturally such matters are in the hands of our English governor. Your affianced husband, in fact."

I wondered what other controlling powers were left in the hands of the local citizens. Since the British had apparently taken over the island without bloodshed, Ian Douglas appeared to have complete control of these people. Did they resent his dictatorial powers as much as I did? Perhaps I might count upon that hostility if I wanted to escape from this paradise.

It was wretchedly hot in the blinding sunlight. I blinked and tried to enjoy the wildly colorful citizenry whose breeches and full skirts, jerkins and blouses, reminded me of a visiting Italian *opéra bouffe.* I could scarcely believe these were real people living real lives. And that among these handsome citizens and their slaves there were many who spied for their rebel leader, Le Maréchal. Was the rebel loyal to his former French masters? Or had this rebellion been spawned against all alien rulers? If the rebel leader operated with the help of French money and other forms of assistance, such as the furnishing of weapons, then perhaps Luc Monceau had agents among the rebels. A frightening thought.

I desperately needed a friend, someone I could trust. My cousin George was a good fellow, but it seemed to me that no secret would be safe with him for long. He might be loyal, but I doubted if he were discreet, especially if he must keep a secret from his admired superior, Ian Douglas! On shipboard I had convinced myself that I might reason with my prospective husband. A period of adjustment had seemed the answer. If Ian Douglas proved to be all that George thought him, my future might become settled and even happy. Out of respect for my husband, love might grow.

But not after this insulting, unthinking behavior which betrayed in Ian Douglas an utter indifference to the woman he expected to make his comrade for life. Shading my eyes when my open-faced bonnet failed to serve its purpose, I looked around again, hoping against hope that George was within hailing distance and that he might help me to find a way out of this. A postponement. Any excuse. Perhaps I could faint. Heaven knows it was hot enough. I should have known better than to wear my deep-blue velvet coat with its close-fitting lines over the bosom and the slim, straight skirts of my new muslin gown. Everything about them was wrong for this climate; even the style, fitted so close to my body, was a disaster.

The spray from the fall of George's rifles as well as the pitch and tar from my brush against the ship's hull had undoubtedly left me an appalling spectacle. I stifled an hysterical giggle at the thought that Ian Douglas might take one look at me and banish me from his sight, and thus solve my problem of obtaining a release from our betrothal.

The town of Port Fleur looked much better on close inspection, in spite of the heat that seemed to descend on us in heavy layers. The gin shops proved to be rum shops. The clapboard structures devoted to shipping stores looked as though they might blow away at the first strong wind. But innumerable little cafés opened onto the semicircular main street and even onto those cross streets which cut upward into the deep green mountains that hovered over the town on three sides. These tiny cafés with their somnolent but brightly clad occupants brought to my memory a happy excursion George and I had made to Paris during the brief Peace of Amiens two years ago, in 1803. The difference was that in Paris the percentage of females at those minuscule tables was greater. Here, as I soon saw, only the European women sat at the tables. Agnes Mabberly headed toward the largest of the cafés below a swinging wooden sign announcing the inn itself: LES DROITS DES HOMMES. I could see that this highly revolutionary sentiment replaced the previous wording: LE ROI BIEN-AIME. I had no doubt that the newly named "Rights of Man" would soon be replaced by a reference to the Emperor Napoleon when the glories of his recent coronation were known here. It said something for Colonel Douglas's generosity, or confidence, that he had not forced the French-speaking natives to Anglicize this colorful and typically Gallic island.

Seeing me look back, Lieutenant Felipe smiled. But his smile was not reassuring; there was contempt in it, and something else. An unsmiling core, I thought.

"You were forced to voyage with such *canaille* as that?"

Surprised, I did not understand for an instant.

"You mean Miss Mabberly?" I saw her motion to a black man in blue-striped breeches and an open jerkin, who was drawing a little wheeled cart full of her boxes and portmanteaux. He vanished into an alley beside the inn, an alley so narrow that the balconies of the inn's upper story and that of a chandler's shop across the way almost touched in an arch overhead. Phoebe and María-Vega came scuffling through the dust behind the cart. The girls wore wide-brimmed, feathered hats like cartwheels, and heavily flounced dresses, the one of green-and-yellow plaid, the other of deep-pink silk. The bottom flounce of each gown, with its less than modish full skirt, dragged the dust along with it.

I resented Felipe's superior attitude. "At all events, they were not so foolish as I was. They did not wear coats."

"How well you and Colonel Douglas will suit!" he murmured, puzzling me by that cryptic remark. But its implication was the first encouraging thing I had heard about the man I was expected to marry.

Now we had reached the little single-story frame building with its two wooden pillars at the doorway. It looked like a child's version of an official building. The word MAIRIE was carved or burned into the wood of a sign over the portal. Tiny though the structure was, it gave the impression of great dignity, even severity. There were no windows on the front. The interior looked pitch dark and forbidding. I wondered if the government of Ian Douglas, or that of his French predecessors, was correspondingly severe.

"Please," I ventured again, hanging back, hoping for any interruption—an act of God, even a volcanic eruption, though I did not believe there were volcanoes on St. Sebastien. "I must wait for my cousin."

But Lieutenant Felipe had already stepped inside the dark interior, and I could not betray any more of this cowardice that would have shamed my parents, and shamed me as well. I straightened my shoulders, set my jaw, and stepped into the Mairie with the aid of the lieutenant's outstretched hand. Once inside, I could see why the place was kept dark: it was also refreshingly cool. I found myself facing an open reception salon of miniature size, but it occupied the entire front of the building and was elaborately, if sparsely furnished with what appeared to be Louis XV pieces, a chair, a settee, a dainty gaming table on which was set a huge vase of scarlet blooms, too overpowering in scent and size for that delicate table.

Directly opposite the entrance, a narrow passage bisected the rear half of the building. The air smelled thickly of a perfume I could not identify. As my eyes became used to the dark, I saw that a faint illumination came from long barred windows at either side of the room. Now there was enough light to see that the perfume came from other flowers, great bowls and vases of freshly cut blossoms, flowers I had never seen before.

A black woman, as tall as I, stood by one of the far windows, arranging some exquisite white flowers so that they floated in a bowl of water. The flowers seemed to glow in the shadowy room.

Lieutenant Felipe said, "Tirsa, I have found the colonel's lady and I bring her to you, quite safe. Mademoiselle Adare, may I present Tirsa to you? She is Colonel Douglas's housekeeper. Tirsa manages the household, both free and slave. She will, of course, take her orders from you hereafter."

The woman was about forty, with worn but still excellent features—hooded, unreadable eyes, and a prominent but not unattractive nose. She was neither friendly nor warm, but had a grace, an elegance that went far to cover any coolness a stranger might find in her. She stepped away from the flowers and curtseyed very slightly to me.

"Mademoiselle? You will be more comfortable in the small parlor adjoining the office of the mayor. Will you follow me, if you please?" She spoke perfect English, rapidly and in a low-pitched tone that suggested a French education.

I thanked her, and she led me through the central corridor to a room at the rear of the building.

"The *salle*—the Room of the Brides," she explained as I caught my breath in dismay, finding myself in a room scarcely larger than a powdering closet and made even smaller by the heavy, suffocating crimson velvet draperies and portières which covered wall and window alike. The room was so stuffy that it smelled of sweating human bodies—not surprisingly, for as French as this room might be, with its careful extinction of all signs of air, it was a perfect repository for heat and stale odors.

"The witnesses have removed from here to the Chamber of Mayor Delafere. You may arrange the hair and bonnet before this mirror if you wish. And should you care to bathe the hands, there is flower water here, and towels."

"Thank you. You are very kind."

The woman nodded and would have departed, leaving me alone in this stifling place, but I called to her, not knowing what I wanted to say, angry that I had been stupid and impetuous enough to find myself in this impossible position.

"I beg your pardon, but there has been a mistake. I had not intended for the ceremony to take place so soon. In fact, I hadn't intended to find myself here at all."

She cut in politely but firmly, "You are Mademoiselle Madeline Mary Adare, the affianced bride of Colonel Douglas?"

"In a manner of speaking, yes. But it was not understood—certainly not by me—that I would present myself here so early. I had expected to have more time."

"Later in the day?" Her dark eyebrows went up. "You wish the ceremony later? But it will be very warm after noon. If I may suggest, it is better while we still have the morning cool."

God help St. Sebastien if this was an example of their "morning cool"! "No. I don't mean this afternoon . . . never mind. I will speak to Colonel Douglas. He does intend to arrive soon, I trust?"

This time she could not miss the edge to my remark, but she avoided it by replying strictly to the letter of my words.

"Naturally, Colonel Douglas will arrive soon. He is hearing a case at the moment. A boy who was running messages for the rebel leader, Le Maréchal, has been captured."

I could not resist the ewer of water she had pointed out, and removing my oil-stained gloves, I set about washing my hands. The water was scented with spring blossoms and I found the result refreshing to my senses and soothing to my nerves. Then I removed my bonnet and tried to make my hair presentable. The ash-blond strands, blown and untidy, looked strange to me after seeing so many brunettes in the town. I attempted to arrange my hair as it had been this morning, in the popular Grecian style, with wisps to lighten the sober look of my forehead and with back curls piled high and released gently over a blue silk fillet. I decided not to put the bonnet on again. I might need all my powers of persuasion to talk Ian Douglas out of this premature wedding.

In the little looking glass I saw Tirsa watching me from the doorway. I remembered suddenly what she had said as she started to leave the room, and I asked, "What will happen to the boy who carried messages?"

"In former days," the housekeeper said without expression, "the boy might have lost his hands . . . if those hands had delivered the messages. Perhaps, in mercy, he might have been executed quickly, with no suffering. You understand, mademoiselle."

I shuddered but then tried to hide the spontaneous gesture of revulsion. I was certain the woman had said these things to arouse just such a reaction in me. I could see her eyes now, fixed upon me, and knew that she despised this unknown Londoner who would be shocked by conduct considered commonplace in these exotic islands.

"And how will my—will the colonel rule in such a case?" I asked. "By the law of former days? Or by a simple execution?"

Tirsa had opened the door but she stopped, frowning, and said after a minute's pause, "By neither alternative." Then she left me, and I heard her calling to various people, issuing orders in French. Apparently she was gathering the group who were to play a part in the wedding of their colonel and governor. I wondered if I would accomplish anything at all by speaking to them, perhaps to the mayor. I felt like one swept into an unknown destiny by fierce winds. There seemed no way to stop myself. But of one thing I was certain: they could not proceed with the actual ceremony unless I cooperated.

When I was reasonably sure that I had done what I

could to make myself presentable, I followed the house-keeper to the corridor outside the airless, blood-colored room. I could hear voices in the room oppo-site. A short, stout Frenchman was about to enter the room with its lively voices, but seeing me, he stopped and bowed politely.

"Mademoiselle the bride, without doubt. I present myself. Raoul Delafere, Mayor of Port Fleur. I shall be delighted to serve on this auspicious day."

I looked around quickly and touched his arm.

"May I speak to you in private, monsieur? I would like to ask your help in delaying—"

"*Parfaitment,* mademoiselle. A delay is planned. For the arrival of the governor. Forgive me, mademoiselle. I am summoned. All must be in readiness." The little man bounced away in answer to a whisper from a pretty native girl who stuck her head out the partially opened door of his office, then disappeared with the nervous official.

I swung around, feeling like an animal in a trap. A furious and panic-stricken animal. The front door was at the far end of the hall—freedom from these insane creatures who seemed determined not to listen to me. Were they all quite mad? And their governor the mad-dest of all?

But he wouldn't conquer me with his ridiculously high-handed tactics! He was not going to play the mas-ter with Madeline Adare, I told myself, the more firmly because I was beginning to feel that all my doubts and fears had been quite inadequate to the real situation. I looked down at my dusty, flat-soled slip-pers that were laced over my ankles in the fashionable new way. I started to walk, first slowly, then in a blind panic, beginning to run. I had almost reached the salon when the voices in the mayor's office grew louder. There was a spurt of laughter that made me look back, wondering if they laughed at me. It was not like me to let such small things trouble me. I must be growing far too sensitive.

A second later I collided with what seemed to be a wall. The impact rattled every bone in my body, and I only prevented myself from falling by a deathlike vise upon the man I had collided with, that impregnable wall! Staring up at him, I knew at once, in spite of my anger and embarrassment, that he was the object of the tempest in the Mairie. That running about, that panic, George's awe—all were caused by the personality of this one man. And they had reason for their fears.

Cousin George had described Colonel Ian Douglas as a big, dark-eyed, handsome man. The image this description conjured up was not quite what I saw before me: a powerful, rude man whose smile at my ridiculous plight was odiously superior, a man who was a little taller than I, but in no way the trim, gentlemanly figure I had hoped for. Soldierly, perhaps. Yes. He was that. But certainly, his eyes would have kept him from ever being described as "handsome." Handsome eyes were gentle eyes, eyes with softness and beauty. Every reader of romances knew that.

Ian Douglas's eyes were the darkest, the most penetrating and fiery, that I had ever seen. Their power was increased by the way he had of narrowing his eyes, so that they almost presented an oblique shape. He was not a man one would like to see in an angry mood. As I stared at him, finding it almost impossible to look away, I recalled Mama's description of a man named Mesmer, whose strange powers had their source in his remarkable eyes.

His hands gripped my arms, and he shook me, not ungently.

"Here, here, don't faint! George promised me you were sound of mind and limb. . . . You *are* my betrothed?"

"Faint? I have never fainted in my life. I assure you, you overestimate your powers if you imagine the mere sight of a rude officer is likely to make me faint!"

Whether deliberately or by chance, the colonel had restored me on the instant with a few casual words. I relaxed my clutch upon his uniform jacket and twisted against his hands, trying to release myself. He let me go abruptly. I could only regard his sense of humor as extraordinary. I felt fairly certain that as he looked down that high-bridged nose of his, he was amused by my indignation. When I could stand without help, I said in cutting tones, "Whatever my other failings, sir, I assure you I am 'sound of mind and limb.' "

"So I see. Yes. Quite sound." This, accompanied by his insulting amusement, simply fired all my complaints.

"I may be your betrothed—I am not quite certain. But I have no intention of being swept into some commitment without so much as a by-your-leave."

"Precisely my feeling. Come along, Madeline . . . it is Madeline—didn't you say, George?"

I had been so dazed by the collision that I did not even realize that my cousin had come in with Douglas. I thought it cowardly of George to let this entire meeting take place without a word of explanation from him. Standing tall and ungainly in the shadows of the salon, he stepped forward, ready enough to speak now.

"Madeline Adare. Yes, Colonel. Madeline has . . . ah . . . a delightful sense of humor. Yes. Humor. Kept us all laughing aboard ship. Can't take her little jests too seriously, I always—"

"George!"

To my surprise, my own angry cry was followed by the colonel's harsh, cutting reproof.

"Adare, stop rambling, for God's sake! Miss Adare, I understand your reluctance. This fool has clearly neglected his duty. Come along."

I could not imagine what the man was about, but as his arm closed about my waist, giving me no choice in the matter, he propelled me along the hall to the noisy group in the mayor's office.

I tried once again. "I hope you have not misunderstood my reluctance to proceed before we are better acquainted, sir."

"Certainly, certainly. Don't hang back."

I felt excessively aware of his arm, tight as a sash about my waist. Warm, too. Uncomfortably warm. Or perhaps it was only the heat of this strange island that disturbed me.

"As long as it is perfectly understood that we must become better acquainted before any decision is made," I said.

He barely glanced at me. "I have said so, have I not? You are to make the acquaintance of all those who will be important in your future."

"And yourself, sir?"

He dismissed this with a bland innocence that illsuited his harsh, dark features.

"But that is the least of your problems. You see how well acquainted we are already?"

"You see?" George echoed behind us.

I looked around, eager to express my frustration to someone who would at least have the good sense to react to my temper—George. "If you have nothing more helpful to contribute, will you be still!" I said sharply.

"George, old boy," Ian Douglas reproved him in his sardonic way, "you failed to describe your cousin's shocking temper."

Unable to release myself, I tried to give him a hard kick, as if by accident. But when my soft-toed slipper met this insufferable soldier's knee-high boot, I suffered more than he did. Even as I groaned I was vaguely aware of another sensation. In my entire life I had never been intimately associated with anyone stronger in nature than the deadly man who haunted me—Luc Monceau. Here at last, I thought, was a man who might be of a more powerful will than Monceau.

Mama had been very beautiful and had got her way by pouting, tears, and occasional illnesses of unspecified origin which departed rapidly when she won her hand. Father had been about equally devoted to what he called "The Good Irish"—his whisky—and his work for Monceau. I was not sure anything in my life had prepared me for the battle of wills between me and this infuriating man.

Keenly aware of Ian Douglas's touch, I suddenly wondered if that touch might not be protective rather than proprietary. Here was a man who could protect me if he were my husband. There was no doubt that his masterful ways might be very attractive to some females. To me they were a challenge. No man had ever mastered me, and certainly this bullying stranger must not be given the upper hand. The difficulty was that he had already begun along this line.

We had reached the mayor's office, and as we three entered, all the chattering stopped. It seemed to me that half of Port Fleur must have squeezed into the room. Even Colonel Douglas seemed surprised at the many faces that turned to stare at us, expectant, excited, and especially so in the case of one man, taller and of lighter complexion than the others. He was Captain Hollin from the *Maud Vester*.

Captain Hollin tried to offer the polite phrases expected on such an occasion, but it was clear to me that this all-too-hasty gathering was the least of his interests. He was obviously eager to impart some piece of news.

"Good day to you again, miss—or as it soon will be, Mistress Douglas." I opened my mouth to deny it, saw his preoccupation with something far more important, and my curiosity as much as any other emotion kept me from correcting him. He said then, "Colonel, you will have heard how the case of rifles came to be lost in the harbor."

"We have discussed it, yes. Captain Adare tells me they may be recovered, though in what condition he is not prepared to say. What now? More difficulty?"

"Would you be good enough to step outside, sir? A little matter about one of my crew."

Colonel Douglas frowned but let me go, and obediently stepped back into the dingy hall with George and the ship's captain. I was left with a chattering crowd of strangers who, embarrassed where I was angry, gathered into a tight little knot and buzzed in French among themselves. Left to my own devices, I remained near the door which was still ajar, while I wondered if I could actually leave here, set up a residence of my own, and be quite independent of that odious Colonel Douglas. The colonel's voice dominated that of the *Maud Vester*'s captain, as I might have expected.

"But damn! How could you let him escape?"

Puzzled and intrigued, I strained to hear Captain Hollin.

"Who would have expected it, sir? My bo'sun tells me that when the fellow was in his cups, he boasted that he had some paymaster from London in his pocket. Some Frenchie was paying him for a favor. He wouldn't say what. Then today, the bastard lets that rifle sling drop and dives in, and nobody's seen him since."

I caught my breath. A Frenchman had hired the sailor—to carry out some favor?

"Frenchies?" George asked in triumph as an idea occurred to him. "Frenchies must want to keep the rifles from reaching us. That Frenchie must be trying to help Le Maréchal and the rebels."

"Aye," the captain agreed. "Very like."

While I listened anxiously, Colonel Douglas said, "It's improbable. But we won't know until we have the sailor caught fast. George, set Lieutenant Felipe and every man we can spare to find the rogue. And take the captain with you. He may have a few ideas. If you'll oblige us, Hollin."

"Aye, sir. A pleasure. Jumping ship, that's one thing I don't hold with. Good day to you, sir. Sorry to've inconvenienced you. Wouldn't dream of putting a wedge in the way of that lovely creature's wedding. You are to be congratulated, Colonel Douglas."

"Rubbish!" said my too frank betrothed. "A matter of social necessity. Some busybodies in the War Office insist I need a wife to entertain the ambitious local women. Organize social affairs, that sort of thing. Tonight, for example. One of those infernal banquets that women delight in. A wife to act as my hostess is absolutely essential, I'm told. It will be the first time the new British command meets the French and the local native aristocracy socially. You delivered the young woman only just in time, Hollin. I assure you, I've no need for a bride, personally, and even less for one of those weak, milk-faced creatures who faint at sight of a cockroach."

While I seethed, Captain Hollin—bless him!—made a gallant defense of me. "Shouldn't think you'll find our Miss Madeline a milk-faced weakling. There's iron in the lady, or I'm a Dutchman."

My cousin George put in hopefully, "Indeed, if I may say so, she is—she is—"

But as I might have expected, Ian Douglas dismissed me and my defenders as of no consequence.

"That's as may be. She might serve her purpose, but she is far from my notion of a strong female who'll weather the hurricanes with me. That other woman you set ashore, that Mabberly. Now there's an old friend. I can count upon Agnes and her girls for the right kind of companionship. My men have been waiting for Mabberly's girls this age. But there is something else, a great deal more important than women. If this Frenchman in London is anxious to aid Le Maréchal, he will hardly do so by destroying a mere score of rifles. What other purpose could he have had in paying your crewmen to drop the load? From what George says, the box damned near brained him and the others in the ship's boat."

I was sure I knew what had been intended. Luc Monceau had a long arm. And somewhere running free on this tiny island was the sailor who had tried to carry out Monceau's order.

Whatever Ian Douglas and I thought of each other— and after his outburst in praise of Agnes Mabberly's girls, I liked him even less—we had a very practical need for one another. My motives were fully as selfish as Douglas's, but I swore to myself in this moment that if I did marry him, he would find me quite as useful, though perhaps in a different way, as he seemed to find Agnes Mabberly.

# 5

During those minutes when Ian Douglas returned to the mayor's office and motioned to me in his proprietary way, I was not quite certain what I should do. I felt that to marry him at once because I badly needed a protector would be cheating. But how would I actually cheat him? Assuming he meant what he had said to the captain of the *Maud Vester,* he did not expect or even desire passion and intimacy from his bride. *Why did I find this disappointing?* He merely wanted a lady to serve as hostess at Government House. That should not be too difficult. After Mama's death I had acted as Father's hostess on many occasions when he wished to ply his guests with the best of smuggled French wines and report their babblings to Monceau.

But if, for reasons of shyness or a secretive nature, Colonel Ian Douglas had lied and actually desired a wife in every sense of the word, a female with the sensuous qualities he expected to find in Agnes Mabberly's girls, what then? To my astonishment, I found this notion not entirely unattractive. I had never thought of myself as a particularly passionate woman. Certainly the London gentlemen who had sought my hand did not arouse in me the passion of fury that Ian Douglas had after only ten minutes' acquaintance. My feelings toward him were nothing if not violent, and though he might be—and indeed, was—an overbearing man, this might make him a successful lover. Perhaps I had always sought a challenging man, one who made me too angry to be bored, too furious to be disdainful. Yes, but not a man so utterly impossible as Ian Douglas. Detestable creature! In addition to every other odious quality, he did not even desire me as a wife.

Of one thing only I was convinced. He would protect his wife from the machinations of Luc Monceau's hireling, that sailor who was now loose somewhere on St. Sebastien to complete his murder attempt.

But as I glanced at Colonel Douglas's profile, I was chilled by a new fear: I was convinced that this man who despised me already would never forgive the treason of which I had been guilty. I could never confess to him what I, and my family, had been. A London court would regard my treason as a serious enough crime, but such a ruthless administrator as Colonel Douglas would undoubtedly judge me as deserving of a hangman's noose. Whatever else came of our businesslike union, he must never know about my treachery or that of my family. If I loathed the memories, and despised myself for having carried on the work after Father died, how then could I bear that a loyal soldier should know of it? The thought was so dreadful that I closed my eyes.

"Here, my girl," Colonel Douglas called to me, "don't look so tragic. You aren't going to the guillotine."

When I raised my head sharply, I saw at once that he enjoyed antagonizing me. Part of that fiery glow in his eyes seemed to be amusement.

"That's better. Delafere has been presented to you? Good. And Tirsa, my housekeeper . . . your housekeeper, after we have signed Delafere's little sheaf of papers here. I suppose it has been explained to you, Madeline. This is a civil service and entirely in French, but happily, a brief affair." He hesitated. "I was informed you do speak French."

"*Certainement, monsieur,*" I said firmly. "*Comme une française.*" Closer to truth than I usually admitted.

Everyone looked at me as though a veil between us had been lifted. I felt that they might eventually admit me to their tight-knit fraternity, which considered itself superior to all of the world's non-French citizens. There were courteous bows, graceful curtseys, all the little gestures that they had failed to show me ten minutes before. I did not mind. I understood the chauvinistic pride that prompted such actions. But of all those who made themselves known to me, I recognized only the quiet, dignified Tirsa and the roly-poly little mayor by sight. I must concentrate upon all the faces, the names. This would be my first duty if I were to help my husband in his task as governor.

Had my decision been made? Should I turn back now? But to go where? There was no practical escape from this union which promised to be violent, wild, and unforgettable. When I was asked to come and stand before Mayor Delafere's desk, I looked around, hoping to catch my Cousin George's attention, but of course, he was off on the hunt for Captain Hollin's missing sailor. I edged away very slowly toward the door, but at exactly the wrong moment Lieutenant Felipe entered.

"The colonel sent for me?"

"Where have you been?" Ian Douglas said impatiently. "You were to join in the search for—" but he abruptly changed his tone, adding with sudden and uncharacteristic politeness, "Lieutenant, you are just the man we need."

Lieutenant Felipe was caught off guard and I thought he looked displeased, but it was difficult to tell from that sleek, smooth face of his. I saw him glance at Tirsa before he said without expression, "As the colonel wishes."

I wondered what relationship there was between him and Ian Douglas's housekeeper. Secret relationships, I had learned long ago, were always worth studying when they involved offices of command like Government House.

"Good. Then we may get on," Colonel Douglas said with enthusiasm, whether real or pretended, I could not tell. "Lieutenant Felipe, you are to act in the capacity of Miss Adare's father. Her witness."

The lieutenant's face stiffened, but when he came to take my arm and I begged his pardon in a hurried whisper, he smiled.

"Not at all, Miss Adare. A rare pleasure."

One could not fault him on his manners.

Under Ian Douglas's eyes, and with an almost indecent haste, Mayor Delafere brought forward his sheaf of papers.

"The marriage contract was signed some months ago by proxy, as I understand it."

I examined the contract. George had signed in my place. Before he had ever discussed the marriage with me, he had signed! These were the insufferable rights of males over females, even males with my cousin's doubtful intellect! It was too late to be furious, though, too late to refuse. I had nowhere to go and no one I could trust. I had made my decision.

Already the mayor was mumbling in French. As a mere bride I had very little to say during this solemnization of vows. I could scarcely believe it when, only three or four minutes later, my hands were being clasped, a dozen voices wished me happiness, Lieutenant Felipe kissed my hand, and finally my husband brushed my cheek with what passed among these Latin witnesses for a proper English kiss. My own promises had been made so unthinkingly, so swiftly, that only now did I wonder about the contents of the marriage contract. I tried to read it amid the bedlam of voices and movement. French wine was being opened, glasses passed around, one of them was thrust into my fingers . . . I need not read all the contract. I knew that in French law my property was now my husband's. But then, Father had seen to that even without Colonel Douglas's added protection of the French marriage contract.

Lieutenant Felipe proposed the toast to the bride. Everyone drank. Then I touched the wine to my lips. A good wine, a Bordeaux. Not the best, certainly, but better than one might expect in this strange little green dot in the rainbow-colored Caribbean. Suddenly the little mayor exclaimed "Grand Dieu!" and set his glass on the desk. We all jumped nervously. He pointed to the big book beside the marriage contract.

"Madame Douglas has not signed the register."

For an instant I puzzled over the identity of Madame Douglas. Then my husband laughed shortly.

"Of course. Quite true. Well, Madeline—give me the pen, Delafere—Madeline, you have one more chance to change your mind." He offered me the long, frayed quill, his eyes dark and penetrating, amused, but . . . what else? . . . a trifle hesitant? Did he actually think I might change my mind?

For the first time in our short acquaintance, I felt that I had the upper hand. I did not prolong the moment. For the benefit of all, I reassured him in French.

"Many thanks, *Monsieur mon Mari*, but I do not change my mind." I scrawled my signature in the register, then remembered and added my married name: "Madeline Mary Adare Douglas."

As if they had all shared my husband's doubt over my reaction, everyone seemed to breathe easier now. They were all acting a trifle drunk on one toast in Bordeaux, an unlikely reaction unless, as I suspected, they had been under a certain tension. Had they? I could not believe that Madeline Adare's signature on a register, or even a marriage contract, was that important to the people of St. Sebastien. Was there something here that concerned me which I did not know about?

After that we drank a good deal of wine in a short period of time. When the supply of Bordeaux had been exhausted, they began on the local rum, a powerful and sweet concoction that I tasted but thereafter avoided. It seemed hours before Colonel Douglas took my arm and then, belatedly, asked if I would care to leave for "my home."

The words had a warm sound. Thoughtful. I wondered whether the effect had been accidental or whether he had chosen the phrase carefully when he called Government House "my home." I must have shown my pleasure because he looked at me suddenly, as though he had not really seen me before, and said, "George neglected to describe your smile." He must have surprised himself as much as he surprised me because neither of us could think of anything to say for a few seconds.

Lieutenant Felipe's smooth voice murmured, "I have taken the liberty of ordering the carriage for your lady, sir, while you examine the Mourne Swamp. We've had a report that Le Maréchal was seen there last night, haranguing the field slaves, and offering the blood of sheep and cocks to the *houngans* for the destruction of the—invaders."

That set Douglas off. "Good God! If you mean the Europeans, say so, Felipe! I am perfectly aware that Le Maréchal regards you blacks as part of his flock."

Felipe said evenly, "I am a renegade, sir. As are all citizens of St. Sebastien who serve the Europeans."

My attention was attracted by the clip-clop of a horse's hooves. I looked out in the street between the surging crowds. An ancient black man in a coachman's caped coat over blue homespun breeches reined in a well-groomed mare, bowed to me, and motioned with his whip toward the carriage seat behind him.

I hesitated, not sure what to do. Ian Douglas stopped arguing with Lieutenant Felipe long enough to dispose of the carriage and me.

"Tirsa will take you to Government House and show you about. If you are not satisfied with your quarters, make any changes you like. And—Madeline—" He was already very free with my name. "You will see to whatever is necessary for the comfort of the guests tonight. The ball will be rather important to the War Office in London, and to my—to our stay on St. Sebastien."

"Certainly. I will be happy to do what I can." His casual instructions suggested to me that he must have been informed of my experience as a hostess in London. At least, I should be good for something here in this strange land. And I was madly determined to be the best and most competent Governor's Lady either my husband or this island had ever seen.

Yet it was maddening to feel helpless, to know that I was being sent off to the unknown house that would be my home for God knew how long! And I was to be sent in the care of a woman who must henceforth take her orders from me. It was not a comfortable situation for Tirsa or for me. I resolved to be especially diplomatic in my encounters with her.

My new husband saluted me and then turned to give orders to Lieutenant Felipe while I watched Tirsa come out of the mayor's office. Her reserve was admirable, but as she joined me in the carriage on the seat opposite and I gave the coachman the signal to start, I found her incurious stare hard to avoid. I remarked upon the beauty of the surrounding mountains.

"I fear they enclose the heat, madame."

"Then I imagine the windward coast is cooler." An inane observation, but I was desperately trying to find a conversational gambit. She gave me the answer my comment deserved.

"Esterby Harbour on the windward coast is windier. It receives the Atlantic currents."

We were passing the most prominent inn of the town and I saw a pert, round-cheeked woman watching our carriage. Agnes Mabberly's red hair shone in the sunlight, and she looked oddly younger now than she had looked in the gray light between-decks of the *Maud Vester*. I waved to her, and asked her how she did. She grinned, waved back, and called out, "Well enough, miss. I always had a fancy for the tropics."

"Very warm," I said, and turning back, caught sight of Tirsa. I had actually shaken her out of her stolid self. She gasped, glanced at Agnes Mabberly, and opened her mouth as if to speak, then closed it abruptly. I had shocked this woman brought up in the formality of Government House. I was a little amused, but did not let her know this.

"We are old friends. We traveled out together from Plymouth," I explained.

Her sense of fitness was so outraged that Tirsa pleated the stiff white·fichu .on her gown with her long saffron-hued fingers.

"Such females will not expect invitations from Government House, madame."

I could not resist the reminder, "That is not very democratic for a product of the French Revolution." Then, as she was clearly offended, I tried to put the matter to rights by joking. I also hoped to cheer myself up after selling my life in a cowardly effort to save it; I despised the manner in which I had yielded to Colonel Douglas's high-handed ways. "Mrs. Mabberly and I shall deal very well," I said. "I have no intention of intruding upon the 'Rights of Man' Tavern, and I am persuaded she has no designs on Government House."

Tirsa's grave expression warned me that she was not amused. So much for my intentions to be diplomatic to the woman with whom I should work closely. Had I done nothing right today?

I hurried to bring up other subjects but failed, and finally surrendered to her mood. I realized now that I had been trying to keep my spirits light because I felt so very depressed. There was no reason for this feeling: Ian Douglas and I had entered into a marriage contract for selfish reasons that had nothing to do with each other's happiness. I reminded myself that I was profoundly grateful to him for making the ceremony a public matter, for intimating ·that his interest in me matched my own indifference to him. Detestable he might be, in his manner, but no promises had been made that good manners and charm would grace my marriage of convenience. I had conflicting impulses. I very much wanted to jump out of the carriage and run—anywhere. Yet I also wanted to show my husband that I was not the nonentity he thought he had married. No passion? No appeal for him? He was going to find out that I could be quite as enticing as Agnes Mabberly. But he would have to earn that passion. He had not married it.

By the time we were on the ascending road to Government House, which bordered the south arm of the bay, I had made a very solemn vow: I would be a good hostess, do my best to win friends for my husband and for his government; I would present, if possible, the perfect portrait of the Governor's Lady. But there would be no intimacy expected or given. We had bought each other, and though I was aware that I had chosen marriage in order to save my life, I did not yet know what Ian Douglas thought he had purchased.

I looked out over the busy harbor with its jungle of masts and the endless colors of water and sailors and brown-skinned swimmers. Despite my agitation, I was keenly aware of all that beauty spread before me. I raised my head to catch my first close view of Government House around the next turn, and at that instant I was nearly blinded by a great, dark, flapping thing that nearly grazed my face, and panicked the horse. Both the mare and I jerked backward. Thanks to the old coachman's steady hand, the mare recovered before I did.

I caught a whiff of something vile, decaying, a nauseating odor combined with the heavy, flailing sound of wings. I slapped frantically at the creature but only succeeded in knocking my quilted taffeta bonnet back on my shoulders, where it hung suspended by the ribbons knotted in a now-strangling bow around my neck.

"What was that?" I gasped. "A bat? It *was* a bat!" I had heard that these creatures lived in the many small but malevolent patches of swamp that crawled over the island.

"A vulture, Madame Douglas. Only a vulture," the housekeeper corrected me, as though this bird were far less sinister than the nocturnal bat. I swung around to look behind me at the town of Port Fleur below. The huge creature, with unexpected color on its wings and hideous beak, had settled in the roadway to gorge on a half-decayed fish dropped by some passerby.

"Vultures in the town?" The moment I had asked this, I regretted my question. It suggested a criticism of my new home, and I wanted very much to be accepted as a good citizen of St. Sebastien. Time enough for criticisms when they regarded me as a friend.

"Vultures, madame, are the cleansers of Port Fleur."

It seemed a highly unpleasant but practical method, and I studied the vulture with renewed interest. The carriage jolted onward. Two island fishermen with a great net slung between them, passed us. Both turned to stare at the carriage. One of the men whispered to the other, and their attention shifted to me. I settled myself in a dignified, straight-backed posture and rescued my bonnet, retying it with fingers that disappointed me by shaking.

And then we were driving up before the east wall of Government House. From the sea the west façade had looked impressive, if forbidding: its great stone foundation was surmounted by the sheer siding of the building with no balconies or overhangs of any kind, and the long windows looked almost medieval in their severity. But here before us, where the dirt road curved past the east entrance, a long wooden terrace with a balcony overhead ran the full face of Government House. Opening onto the terrace were many long windows that suggested public rooms—a ballroom and salons, probably. Overhead there were similar pleasant windows, giving ventilation for the bedchambers, I hoped.

Government House looked to be considerably larger and more splendid than Adare House in London, and what was more daunting, I would have the native population, including slaves, to deal with as household servants. Everyone of any consequence in England and France believed slavery to be an evil that must eventually be stamped out. Laws were forever being proposed. But here in this outpost of the older civilized world, the institution seemed to be endemic to the life and the land. I did not know how to handle such matters. It was a far cry from the single housekeeper and scullery maid with whom I had managed Adare House.

"Madame?" Tirsa said politely. "We have arrived. Shimbé, see to Madame."

The mare had evidently been well trained. The old coachman wound the reins into a loop and dropped them on his high perch. Then, with some rheumatic difficulty, he climbed down and approached me. I tried to give him no trouble in descending, and learned one of my first lessons in getting on with the people of my husband's domain: they all had their appointed tasks, and one must take care to let them perform these tasks, however useless or difficult, or even simple, they might be.

The old man saw me step down without his assistance. After thanking him, I walked briskly toward the terrace. I was aware of his watery, faded eyes watching, and more keenly, of Tirsa's gaze, her intense interest in everything I did.

It was beastly hot, and I would be relieved to step inside what I hoped was a cool house with ventilation spreading through the west windows high over the bay to the east drive where we stood. I tried to open the latticed door, but Tirsa hurried in front of me and seized the brass knocker which was shaped— unpleasantly, I thought—like a serpent's head. I tried, though I expect I failed, to give the impression that I was naturally indifferent to custom. I half expected to be greeted by another ancient, creased black face like that of Shimbé, the coachman, but instead, a slender, pretty young girl came to welcome me. She put me in mind of someone, but I could not place the resemblance. There was a quick, lithe look about her, and she moved with a silent animal grace.

Tirsa said, "This is Pepine, who will attend you. Lieutenant Felipe tells me you are not accompanied by your own maid."

"No." Although a personal maid was necessary to give countenance to a single young woman living alone, a maid in my former profession would have been a disaster: there are no secrets from one's own abigail. So I lied quickly, as I had lied to the surprised captain of the *Maud Vester*. "My maid remained in Plymouth," I said. "She suffered from the dropsy, and found she could not travel. I was forced to leave her in the care of her sister. I miss her sadly, but perhaps Pepine will do."

Pepine dipped a brief curtsey and led me into the house. The central hall smelled of old wood, long in the sun, but there was also a scent of rotting wood, and I wondered how wild the sea could become during a storm. Thanks to its foundations, Government

House stood above the water, but during hurricanes the spray and rain would saturate the house. And in a gale it would be the highest target on the leeward coast of St. Sebastien.

I had spent my life under tension and suspicion. I had learned early to trust no one. For that reason I was trained to notice even the smallest nuances of emotion around me. I noted now, while appearing unconscious of the byplay, that Tirsa and the young Pepine made certain signals to each other. I guessed that Tirsa was dramatizing my type and temperament to the younger woman, informing her what to expect of me.

Well enough. I understood that. But I was on my guard—indeed, I could not recall a time when I had not been on guard. Still, I smiled pleasantly at Pepine and followed her through the house toward the suite of rooms that she told me had been set aside for "the Governor's Lady." We climbed the central staircase, a shadowed but impressive flight up to an open hall that hung like a spying balcony over the entrance hall below. This upper hall was decorated with portraits, all of them French in style which seemed to represent previous governors of St. Sebastien. But both the artistry (or lack of it) of the paintings, and the planning of Government House itself, suggested that no one in Paris or Versailles had devoted his best efforts to this obscure island in a far-off, rainbow-colored paradise.

I saw that this open hall abovestairs was the only connection between the north and south wings of the building. No movements could be made between the family's private quarters without being known to the most casual of visitors in the main entrance hall below. Nonetheless, I was relieved to discover that a certain amount of fresh air circulated among these rooms, from west to east, and I remarked on the fact to Pepine, whose lively sloe eyes observed my every reaction.

"It is very comfortable, this house," she agreed. "A pity it is not lucky. Very nice for Governor Douglas. But for wives in the Caribbean, not so lucky."

I resented what I sensed was a deliberate effort to discourage me, but I did not let this show. As we started toward the north wing, I said, "The governor's quarters are at this end of the building? Are they private, or does he use any of the salons up here for public conferences?"

"It is Madame's suite we go to now, not the governor's. Here in this corner, with windows opening upon the north and west. Across the hall, the bedchamber on the east is unoccupied. It was formerly the chamber of the late governor's . . ."

I was surprised, and wondered, too. "But if it was the governor's lady who slept there, why is it not my chamber?"

"Not the Governor's lady, madame, but the late French governor's mistress. Ah! Here is your door. Very cool in here, I think, with the breeze from one window to the other. Monsieur the Colonel thought of this when he had it prepared for you. The colonel is very thoughtful."

"Very thoughtful, indeed." Considering the change in national government here, it was good to know that the people of St. Sebastien respected my husband. I stepped into a charming little sitting room furnished in delicate French pieces: a chaise longue with only slightly faded green satin cushions, an exquisite little escritoire, and a commode of ebony and oriental lacquer, designed with strange, entwined serpents in gold. Above the commode was a large, gold-framed looking glass. I saw myself reflected there, my hair disheveled, my bonnet ribbons crookedly tied, my coat still stained with salt water from the fall of those rifles into the bay.

"Heavens!" I exclaimed, removing the bonnet and grimacing at the reflection there, "what a sight to see on one's bridal day!"

Over my shoulder I saw Pepine's thin, dark face. She smiled at my remark, obviously agreeing with me. Catching my eye, she quickly turned, opening the door behind her into the bedchamber.

"Your boxes were delivered while you and the Governor were signing the marriage contracts, madame."

I thanked her and entered the pleasant green and gold bedchamber, noting the extremely feminine bed across the room. A miniature canopy fell from gold serpent carvings overhead, and the green bed curtains hung in light, airy folds, concealing nothing of the bed except the bolsters at its head. Thus the tropic night air might circulate, relieving the heavy heat.

"Darielle, who is one of the household, unpacked your boxes and portmanteau. She believed you would prefer your—night cordial at your bedside."

"Night cordial!" I looked at the beautifully carved little bedside stand with its tapered candle in a silver holder. Beside the candlestick was an ugly little bottle, squat and dark, carefully wiped free of sand and cobwebs. Such bottles were brought into England by the free traders from France during the blockade, having escaped the English excisemen. It was exactly like the bottles of excellent French brandy which Luc Monceau served while collecting information from my father, or later, from me. It was not a bottle I had put into my baggage.

This was Luc Monceau's way of saying, "I know where you are. I will bide my time, but in the end I will destroy you."

# 6

In spite of my best efforts, I must have revealed my shock. I caught Pepine watching me closely as I examined the bottle.

"Where did you say it was found?"

"In Madame's portmanteau."

Easily enough reached. Had the bottle been deep in my largest box of clothing, I would suspect it had been placed there in England, but anyone might open the portmanteau and put it in—anyone on the island, any one of the ship's crew. It would have to have been done since I packed the portmanteau immediately after breakfast.

"Who delivered my things?"

A little thread of a frown crossed her unlined forehead. "But a sailor from your ship, madame. Who else?"

"Did he carry my things into Government House? I mean to say, was he in a hurry, or did he remain to assist?"

"He did not remain, madame. He said he was in great haste. He was needed aboard the ship."

I considered the bottle. "When he left the house did he return by way of Port Fleur, or did he go on around the drive toward the south of the island?"

Pepine shrugged. She gave every indication of being

about to deny any knowledge at all, but suddenly she laughed, still puzzled.

"It is very strange. He did not return to Port Fleur. He continued around the drive with his cart and disappeared. The drive runs to the South Coast Road and another that crosses the south half of St. Sebastien, close by the great Boiling Lake, which is in the middle of the island. Why did he not return to the ship?"

"Why indeed?" I echoed. "Take this bottle and destroy it."

"Destroy!"

"One should never drink gifts from unknown donors." It was unfortunate that I had made so much of the matter; I did not dare speak of the sailor to Colonel Douglas, nor did I wish the sailor captured alive. He might even know of my espionage activities. As for the "gift" itself, Luc Monceau must know that I would not be so foolish as to drink the contents. I would surely guess where that bottle came from, for it was so like those others he received from the free traders. No. It had been a warning to me, a taunt that he had not forgotten me. I was still within his reach.

Pepine appeared doubtful about destroying a bottle of good brandy, so I reached for it again. "Let me do it then. Where is the powdering closet? Or shall we go down to the kitchen? Is there a kitchen in the house, or is it a separate building?"

"There is a stillroom at the south end of the house, on the ground floor. Much of the cooking for the banquets—for tonight, for instance—is done over the fires in the pits beside the kitchen house."

"It doesn't matter," I said, and went to the long windows overlooking the bay far below. Pepine unlatched the window and pushed it open, and I tossed out the bottle. We both looked out after it, following its descent until it neatly struck the blue waters then sank beneath them.

"It looked very nasty," Pepine said after a little silence between us.

"Not in its original state." She stared at me, and I rapidly retreated from this hint that something had been added to the brandy. "That is to say, not when it was first smuggled over to the Sussex coast."

"I see, madame," she said, but I suspected that she did not. I then told her that we must postpone the further examination of Government House until I had changed, and having thanked her, I thought I might be alone for a blessed half-hour. But Port Fleur was not London, and when the nervous little maid Darielle came in with a basin of water in which, presumably, I was to wash my entire body, she was soon followed by two more maids, giggling but otherwise silent. All three were to assist me in my dressing. When I saw that my own preference for privacy would only cause havoc in the household, I yielded, fearing a precedent would be set, as indeed it was.

I suggested examining the public rooms, but was told that my presence would sadly discommode the household staff and the free town workers hired for the occasion of the reception and dinner. The long dining salon was still strewn with chairs, newly polished silver candelabra, and baskets of incredible flowers. I volunteered to arrange the flowers, and since none of the busy workers was in a position to refuse me, I filled several vases and set them on the sideboard to be placed on the long table later. Unhappily for my confidence in my own ability to supervise a grand occasion, I discovered an hour before the evening's reception began that all the flowers had been replaced in native wooden bowls, with exquisite floating petals and leaves. Far lovelier and more appropriate than my stiff English or French methods. I had an entire lifetime of things to learn, in a world which was as strange to me as the deserts of China.

The business of the flowers was small, but it pointed out my enormous inadequacies in this new world. I reminded myself that I owed a great deal to my unknown and obviously indifferent husband. I had dreaded a physical relationship with a repulsive stranger, but had instead been given my own suite and a surprising degree of freedom thus far. Therefore, I must make up to him in other ways for the shortcomings of our marriage. He had made it quite clear that I was to be decorative, well-mannered, and provide the social link between the military government and the citizens of St. Sebastien. It would be a point of honor for me to oblige him. Nevertheless, I wondered what it would be like to be loved by this tempestuous man. I found myself envying Agnes Mabberly and hurriedly turned my thoughts to more practical matters.

Knowing the importance of that first evening to my new husband, I resolved to demonstrate at once that as his wife I would be an asset. But as the afternoon passed all too quickly and I found myself within half an hour of appearing to receive the first arrivals, I began to doubt everything about myself. I had seen nothing of my husband since the hasty ceremony in the Mairie, and his absence put me on my mettle. He would see me tonight, by heaven!

I debated over the wearing of my finest gown, which I had originally ordered for an important naval reception at the house of the old admiral who lived across the square from Adare House. My usual task was to listen to gossip, while flirting with the naval guests. It was an idea increasingly repulsive to me. How satisfy-

ing to wear that gown now for such an opposite purpose!

The gown was of exquisite green silk with a golden
gauze overskirt and shawl. I would wear the emerald
earbobs that Mama's mother had worn at the court of
the aging Louis XV, and I would see if one of my
numerous maids could help me to pile my hair into
the formal Grecian mode, partially confined by a
green ribbon fillet. My kid slippers of that same leaf-
green shade were somewhat worn, but I managed to
make them presentable by vigorously polishing them
with silver paper before the maids came to help me. I
thought I understood the value represented by my
wardrobe. I wondered if the citizens of St. Sebastien
knew that my inheritance would be managed by my
husband.

I wondered also, as I was being dressed, whether
even my husband had precise information about my
estate. Did George? If so, I had no doubt that Ian
Douglas had known before making the offer for me.

With a good deal of apprehension I inspected the
image put together by three maids and myself. I tried
not to think now of how important this night, and the
actions of the new governor's lady, might be to my
husband and to the people of St. Sebastien. I told myself to imagine that the reception and the dinner were
like those at which I had presided scores of times, as
Father's hostess and later as my own mistress. But how
different and how wonderful to remember that if I
succeeded as hostess tonight I need not be ashamed of
my accomplishment, as I had so often known shame
when I worked for the French agents in London!

We women were all startled by a male voice. In the
doorway between my sitting room and bedchamber,
my cousin George presented himself, claiming that he

had knocked but we were chattering too loudly to hear him. He looked neat and handsome in his gaunt way.

"Change of duty, cuz. Colonel says I'm to provide an escort to one of the local beauties. Thought it might be you, but old Ian said no. I say! Not bad, cuz. Not bad at all."

His admiration would have been pleasant if the sight of him hadn't reminded me of his assignment that afternoon.

"Whatever happened to the fellow you were pursuing, George? The sailor, or whoever he was."

"Sailor. Yes. We'll have the fellow snug in the brig by the time the colonel's banquet is done. He'll tell us why he tried to kill me with that box of rifles, or by gad, he'll wish he had told us!"

Two of the three girls eyed George's scarlet-jacketed length adoringly, but Pepine made me uncomfortable because she glanced at me as George spoke, and I realized, too late, that I had nervously broken an ivory stick of my fan.

I said hurriedly, "I imagine Colonel—my husband will expect me. The first carriages will be arriving soon. George, will you give me your arm?"

"Nothing easier, old girl. Here. You're trembling. Not frightened of a few Frenchies and blacks, are you? Why, I've seen you master a hundred parties like this at Adare House."

I attempted a smile that flickered on and off as we moved through the upstairs hall. A pair of commonplace but practical oil lamps provided the sole illumination for the hall. I could not imagine where the scent of perfume came from, but soon discovered that all household odors were disguised by the plenitude of tropical flowers placed in odd nooks and corners.

I let George think my sudden fit of nerves was due to the approaching banquet, but my head whirled with fears of what the murderous sailor would confess, under the proper circumstances. Try as I would to concentrate upon other matters, such as the approaching parade of curious and critical guests as well as my husband's first view of his wife without mud and water stains, I kept returning to that particular fear: did the sailor know why he had been hired to kill me? And if he did, would he confess? What happened to women found guilty of my crimes? Were they hanged, drawn and quartered like all traitors?

I shuddered, and George said, "What? Not nervous again! I believe you are chilled. Brace up. They can't eat you." And to my surprise—for George was anything but romantic—he added, "Not but what they'll want to eat you, old girl! Never realized what a devilish good figure you present when you are half naked."

I hurriedly raised the gauze shawl which had fallen to my shoulders, but after that unexpected comment I felt remarkably bare below the shoulders. However, my gown was quite correct in London and Paris, and I must try to bear that in mind if the local ladies attempted to make me a pariah.

We had reached the landing when we heard carriage wheels creak over the ground, coming to a halt before the square wooden pillars that gave dignity to the portico.

"Rented carriages. The normal transportation is the bare foot," George muttered in my ear. A shadow crossed the glittering lights of the candelabra that lined the hall below, and I caught my breath, hoping the tension did not show in my face.

The butler of Government House took long, deliberate steps to the portico where lesser household attendants waited to greet the guests and aid in the removal of the carriages. I moved away from George and leaned over the carved balustrade to catch a glimpse of our first guests. I was in this undignified position when a laugh, masculine and contagious, startled me. Ian Douglas had followed the butler toward the double doors but stopped to look up at me. I straightened slowly and managed to smile.

"I am afraid, sir, you caught me spying." I wished at once that I had not used quite that word, but it went unnoticed. Taking George's arm, I walked down the last flight of stairs while, to my satisfaction, my husband stared up at me with the most flattering but nerve-racking intensity.

As we reached him, he took my hand, nodding to George. Unoffended, my cousin sauntered off to exchange a few words with Tirsa, standing somber and handsome in the entrance to the ladies' withdrawing room. Ian Douglas still looked at me. I felt my body grow faintly heated under that scrutiny until the mingled sounds of voices on the portico put him in mind of his duty. But he was good enough to tell me teasingly, "I see I have acquired a greater bargain than I had any right to expect in a wife."

I wished he would not speak of bargains. Such talk reminded me again of the businesslike nature of the bond between us, and inevitably it also made me think of the missing sailor who might destroy me at any time by a few words.

Nonetheless, the colonel's compliment cheered me considerably, and when he pressed my fingers in his hand, which was lean and hard and not at all gentle, I flashed my warmest smile. I think he was disturbed for an instant or two before his dark eyebrows raised in that sardonic way I had first noticed. Then he tucked my arm into his and slowly strolled with me to the wide section of the hall in front of the public salons. Before we turned our backs to these rooms I caught a glimpse of them, simple in construction to the point of austerity but bathed in the golden glow of numerous wall sconces and candelabra. The luster of crystal gave a diamond-like sparkle to the farther room seen between the long double doors. That would be the dining salon, I recalled. I saw Tirsa and smiled, nodding to her. She returned my nod with a curtsey. Somberly beautiful as she was, I felt that she must be justifiably proud of tonight's work.

A woman so attractive now must have been very beautiful indeed a few years ago, during the French rule, and I remembered Pepine saying that the French governor's mistress had slept in the rooms across the hall from my suite. Had Tirsa been here in those days? Her education was certainly French. How had she enjoyed serving that mistress who was probably no more handsome than she?

"My dear Madeline—"

My husband's voice stirred me to present matters. As usual it held a hint of sarcasm—light, cutting, yet impossible to pin down as hostile. "Let me present Monsieur and Madame Yvon de Castries. The Castries Sugar Mills are certainly our greatest asset on St. Sebastien."

I smiled lavishly, and watched my hand—or the air slightly above my hand—lightly kissed while Madame curtseyed. Madame was black, heavy-set, but magnificently gowned in a style made popular some years ago by the Vicomtesse de Beauharnais, recently become the Empress Josephine. Unhappily, Madame de Castries did not possess the Empress's svelte figure, but she was impressive nonetheless, and had an air of great dignity. Her husband, the sugar mill king, was about half her size, a little cockerel who, nevertheless, appeared to be a man to reckon with.

After that, the guests came rapidly. My smile froze on my face: "Too kind, monsieur . . ." "Yes, a whirlwind courtship, indeed . . . !" "Thank you, madame. You are very kind. . . ." "No, madame. It is I who am fortunate. Your lovely rainbow of a world has quite captivated me. . . ." "Too kind, Captain . . ." "Mrs. Copeland? Yes, indeed. I know of your accomplishments. My dear Colonel Douglas has spoken of the work you and Mr. Copeland have done for St. Sebastien!"

Once, when we took a breath between presentations, my husband bent toward me. Tickling my ear with his lips, he murmured, "I congratulate you on your skill. How do you know what to say to each of them?"

Memory, and the reason for my skill, saddened me, but I said lightly and honestly, "Long experience, Monsieur le Colonel. Quite simple, really."

He gave me a troubling look that penetrated deeply: it made me wonder how much he did know of me.

"I think you may, in perfect propriety, address me as Ian."

Without trying to play the coquette, I confessed, "I am afraid propriety does not replace a reasonable acquaintance. After all is said, we *are* strangers, Colonel." But when he frowned, I rested my fingers briefly on his hand. "From strangers we may move to friends. Isn't it so?"

He gave no indication that my touch had softened his hard, jesting manner. "You speak French like a

Parisienne. I suspect you are going to be a treasure to me in my work, Madeline. You see how easy it is to use familiar names?"

I laughed and promised to try and remember. His alarming dark eyes examined me again. I might have been one of Agnes Mabberly's girls after all. The sensation was curious. Degrading, yet intensely pleasurable. I was shaken by the realization.

Fortunately for my poise, a British officer and a beautiful young mulatto woman arrived then, were greeted, and at last we were permitted to go in to dinner, where I was enormously relieved to be able to sit down. I was beginning to suffer from simple physical exhaustion after disembarking from the ship that morning, barely missing a violent death from the falling rifles, finding myself married without a by-your-leave, and finally, faced with this long reception.

All the same, the dinner was a success, thanks in great part to Tirsa's supervision of the food and the decorations. The fare was lavish, yet pleasantly light. I was unused to the succulent seafoods served throughout each course, and scarcely more acquainted with the vegetables and fruits which appeared and disappeared in bewildering varieties. The fruits in particular were exotic to me—tender vermillion-colored crescents, biting and memorable, soft green-skinned globes, and brown-skinned bananas which I had seen served once in London, each with a marvelous and individual taste. It was all too much. I was surfeited with these riches in a land whose work was almost entirely in the hands of slaves. I wondered if the slave diet profited at all by these products of their labors.

There were no discussions of such matters, although I had been hostess in London upon several occasions when abolition was loudly advocated. Here in St. Sebastien, the subject was never alluded to. However, much time was spent in congratulating Colonel Douglas upon his excellent selection of the wines served. Seeing my expression, my husband remarked with cool amusement, "Even the British occasionally have moments of taste."

Every Englishman present laughed. The black and French guests exchanged glances, and explanations traveled tortuously down the length of the table. Except for Ian Douglas's remark, which I assumed was a rebuke to me, there was no unpleasantness. While the gentlemen drank their after-dinner Madeira, I found the ladies of St. Sebastien very like women of the privileged class everywhere. I need not have feared my fashionable gown was shocking, there was far more exposure of flesh in the case of many of these women. But it seemed to me that the climate encouraged languorous ease—and corpulence, which was revealed in the deep-bosomed, diaphanous gowns with their lack of petticoats. The women were talkative, curious, and quite ready to accept me on a temporary basis, subject to my future behavior. I determined to win them over by that behavior. Sometime during that long but worthwhile evening, I knew I wanted to be accepted by these people, including my husband, as I had never wanted anything in my life.

By the time we stood on the portico, attending the departure of the governor's guests in the homely way of many a husband and wife, my spirits were remarkably lifted.

"It seems to have gone very well," I said, when the last horseman had trotted his mount off beside the open carriage of Mayor Delafere and his petite French wife. Madame Delafere was noticeably interested in the mounted soldier while the roly-poly little mayor revealed what I considered bad tactics by dozing off. I had made my remark to Colonel Douglas more or less mechanically, as I might have done years ago to my father when the guests had drifted down the staircase and out to their waiting carriages. It was, therefore, something of a surprise when my husband seized upon this prosaic remark.

"Do you know, you are an extraordinary woman?"

"How so?"

"You did not say what any other bride would: 'How did I do?' or 'Do you think they liked me?' or some such silliness. You spoke of the dinner as though it were a business matter."

"But was it not?"

"Precisely. All the same, most women would not have cared a farthing for the success of the evening. Their own triumph or failure would have been much more to the point."

I smiled. "I must disappoint you, then. I was very hopeful of my own success."

But he would not have it so. He was determined to be generous, and I would not have been female if I hadn't been intensely aware of him, of the fiery look that was belied by his quick, sardonic humor which cut through pretension and pomposity. Yet even the pompous and pretentious were capable of being hurt, and I wondered if it were this habit that had caused him the trouble in the War Office at which George had hinted.

"Yes, you are remarkable," he said. "And I find you mysterious for that reason."

This dubious compliment almost made me laugh. "You find me mysterious for such a reason? Forgive me, but you cannot have known many females if that is your reasoning."

"You forget. I was married before. For a brief but
. . . memorable time. Beauty can be as superficial and
unsatisfying as a paper skin. My wife feared every dinner, despised every friend of mine, hated every officer.
She understood nothing whatever about me and would
never learn."

"And you?" I asked. "Did you try to understand
her?"

He blinked. Apparently he wasn't used to being
questioned. But I was glad to note an innate sense of
fairness in this explosive man.

"No, I suppose not. She was very young. We had
nothing in common. I tried—" He caught the little
smile I quickly suppressed, and shrugged. "Well, I did,
all the same! But she wouldn't have me."

"All women are not the same, sir."

He stared, then said, "Maybe not. But I haven't married all women." He turned away abruptly and would
have left me there upon the portico where servants
were quietly taking down the hanging lamps, but I
opened my fan, waved it before my flushed face, and
said to him, "You are quite right. It has been a long
day."

Recollecting his manners, he looked back, offered
his arm, and we went inside together. I was deathly
tired and in a state of nerves as well, thinking of what
a disaster an attempt at lovemaking might be tonight,
for me, at least. This man, whose sensual appeal was
obvious to me already, would be demanding, a quality
which had always seemed to me ideal in a husband of
his attractions. But after all the events of the day, I
was not at all sure I could satisfy him tonight. He
would, perhaps, be confirmed in his low opinion of
the female sex, and I might have a difficult time dis-
proving that fixed view.

90

Tirsa came and wished us goodnight. I thanked her for the splendid success of the evening and succeeded at last in sparking a flicker of warmth, even pleasure, in her face as she accepted my praise.

"Madame is generous," she murmured, and when Ian Douglas had added his thanks to mine, she curtseyed and left us.

My husband and I climbed the stairs. From the upstairs hall, I glanced down to see Tirsa standing in the doorway of the small salon, where she had stopped to watch us. She was obviously interested in our marital conduct. My arm trembled slightly in his, and I set myself the stern task of showing no sign of uneasiness.

At the door of my suite he asked me if I found my rooms comfortable. Flustered by all his formality, I replied that they were exquisitely furnished and that I was happy with them. He released my arm, and while I stood there looking, I daresay, as foolish as I felt, he took my hand. He seemed to examine it, or perhaps only the plain gold band he had placed on it earlier that day. Then he kissed my fingers lightly, and bade me goodnight. I could have sworn there was a glint of amusement in his face as he turned away.

I went inside my sitting room, hardly knowing whether my reaction was relief or a sharp and humiliating disappointment.

What is worse, Pepine and one of the other young maids were waiting to remove all my finery, and they knew quite well what had happened. I made what I hoped was a good pretense that this was a normal state of affairs, and my performance was aided by Pepine's elaborate delivery of a note to me on a little pewter plate. Soon my thoughts had fled from my husband's strange behavior.

"What is this?"

"It was delivered during the reception, madame. The woman said you would recognize the name."

Since I could not think of any woman I knew on St. Sebastien, I was puzzled and examined the paper briefly before unfolding it. I could see that anyone, including Pepine herself, might have opened it.

The few lines within were written in a fair hand and the words spelled correctly.

*"Miss Madeline—you were good to my young ladies and me when we thought to die in that horrid ship.*

*"Ma'am, one of my young ladies, Maria-Vega, was this evening the guest of a local free man of color at a cabin in the Mourne Swamp north of town.*

*"You will remember the sailor, Peter Phipps, of the* Maud Vester, *who dropped the load of rifles upon us? Maria-Vega tells me Phipps stumbled into the cabin hoping to get help from her gentleman. Phipps had caught a bullet from the Governor's soldiers who were after him, but he managed to evade them. Maria-Vega's gentleman let Phipps stay, but Phipps keeps babbling that you were his target in that accident on shipboard today. I thought you should know.*

*"I would have written this to my old friend, Colonel Douglas, but I felt you would wish to tell Ian yourself.*

*"I hope I may sign myself your friend, Agnes Mabberly."*

Pepine's voice startled me. "Will Madame require a messenger?"

"A messenger? Why?" Had she read the note? I suspected so, but I could not be certain.

Pepine shrugged. "Only that I recognized the man who brought it. He works in the town. Upon occasion he has delivered messages from Mayor Delafere or Madame Delafere."

"Thank you," I said. "No messenger will be necessary." I held the paper over the flame in the nearest lamp.

But half an hour later, when I lay down for the first time in the large, comfortable bed and tried to sleep, I kept wondering what that sailor, Peter Phipps, would be forced to tell about my past if I gave the note to my husband. I had much rather remain in physical danger from Phipps than to have Ian Douglas capture him and perhaps hear the truth about me.

# 7

Of course, I awoke in the night, haunted by the question I should have asked before exhaustion and panic had driven me to burn the message from Agnes Mabberly. I lay there in the warm, airless room, turning from one side of the bed to the other, hoping to find some spot of coolness.

Agnes Mabberly knew my husband. They were old friends. *Friends?* And if no one appeared tomorrow to seek out the wounded sailor, Peter Phipps, Agnes would certainly wonder why I had not told my husband about her message. Then, upon her first meeting with Colonel Douglas, she would undoubtedly ask if they had captured the wounded Phipps at the cabin in Mourne Swamp. And then would follow the information that I had known the whereabouts of the fugitive and neglected to inform my husband. By destroying the paper and keeping silent, I had merely added proof to the charge the fugitive might make against me, a charge that would send me to the gallows.

I could not sleep. I had dozed off earlier, aching in every bone, and fatigued from my brain to my toes, but now that I had awakened, my problems would not vanish. The question of Agnes Mabberly's letter refused to be solved. I got out of bed and felt my way to the long windows. At my suggestion the shutters had been left open on the window that opened onto the water, and the blue dark poured in across the blessedly cool, uncarpeted floor, giving the room a faint semblance of light. At the window I could see stars everywhere, I had never guessed so many existed. Directly below my windows the waters of the bay glimmered. Little native piraguas floated over those waters, and in the distance, inside the bay of Port Fleur, the horizon was crowded with black sticks, geometric in their patterns—the bare masts of ships at anchor.

I opened the window, then went to the next and pushed it open. Whatever the superstitious natives of St. Sebastien might think about night air, I wanted a fresh current in this stifling room. Perhaps I could then think more clearly about the problem of Agnes Mabberly's warning. Certainly the salt breeze that fanned my face was welcome now.

I found my robe, which I had flung across the foot of the bed, and then I located my green evening slippers where I had left them by the armoire. I stepped into them and made my way through my bedchamber and the sitting room toward the hall beyond. But absurdly enough, I had no notion where my husband slept. I considered for a minute or so, then went back to the worn, petit-point bellpull beside the commode and summoned whoever among the servants might be on night duty.

When I received no response I looked into the hall, which was alive with tiny sounds: the creaking of wood, the faint flutter of the lamplights in the rush of sea air from the open windows of my bedchamber, and a sound closer at hand. Someone was in the opposite bedchamber, the room that, according to Pepine, had once been occupied by the mistress of the French governor. I would not have been surprised at this hour to see the ghost of that mistress looking much like the late Madame Du Barry.

I was rapidly retreating when the door of that room opened and the housekeeper, Tirsa, stepped out. She was fully dressed in neat black with full skirts and a spotless white fichu crossed over her shapely bosom. At sight of me, she caught her breath.

"Madame?"

"I am sorry to disturb you at this hour," I began, postponing as long as possible the humiliating disclosure that I did not know where my husband slept on our wedding night. "I have some important information about a—a criminal matter. Will you please inform Colonel Douglas's valet that I must speak to the colonel when he wakes?"

She had more self-possession now, and even managed a little smile that I found annoying until the shock of her next words blurred the original offense.

"That should be very simple, madame. I have just seen Colonel Douglas returning from Port Fleur."

"At this hour! A duty at this hour?" I hurried into the east bedchamber. It was unfurnished now, but the careful moulding of the white room, and the green-and-gold wallpapering showed good taste on someone's part. I looked out the closed window just in time to see my husband dismount from a rough-looking black horse. He gave over the reins to a waiting boy and disappeared within the portico.

I became aware of breathing just behind me. Tirsa stood there, also looking down. I whispered sharply, "I have a message for him. An important matter about something that happened on shipboard. Agnes Mabberly was on board, and told me—"

"Agnes Mabberly, madame? Then you need have no concern. Colonel Douglas has spent some time with

Mrs.—with that female tonight. She will have given him the message, surely."

It was a blow, and not only to my pride. In that second I hated both Tirsa and Agnes Mabberly. With an effort I managed to shrug off the shock of the news that my husband had spent our wedding night with a prostitute and her women.

"In that event," I said, "he can scarcely need my assistance. Mrs. Mabberly will have given him the information directly. Good night again, Tirsa."

She did not seem to hear me. She remained in the room, apparently staring out the window at the darkened town in the distance. I left her there and returned to bed. Surely Agnes Mabberly would have informed Ian Douglas about the location of the fugitive sailor. As for the sailor's possible accusations if captured, I would admit to having known a Frenchman named Luc Monceau. It had always been my habit to tell the truth whenever possible. I hoped the acquaintance might be accepted as natural, since one of my parents had been French. The matter of my spying, I would deny. I had hoped that someday I might know my husband well enough to confess the truth. Whether he would despise and punish me, or whether he might understand and forgive, I probably could not guess for a very long time. In the circumstances, it seemed likely that we would never know each other.

Meanwhile, as I plumped up my pillows and tried once more to sleep, I thought it very possible that I might end by being sent back to England—once I had served as Ian Douglas's respectable wife and hostess, but only in public. I slept eventually, and dreamed of horrid phantoms floating over swamps while I sank, choking in the oozing mud. I had not seen the Boiling

Lake, but in my imagination it already existed as a familiar nightmare region.

I awoke late, disappointed that I had not risen at a respectable hour so that I could learn more about the household. I was awakened finally by the humid heat that already clung to my body, and for a moment, before I opened my eyes, I was confused.

The room appeared to be firm and solid. The bed did not sway. The air, while it carried a hint of salt that I remembered all too well from the *Maud Vester,* was also flower-scented. I was in my husband's house. I opened my eyes in that lovely, spacious room and thought that in the morning light it was the prettiest room I had ever seen. I was happy.

But almost at once the old worries crowded in: my awful, gnawing guilt over the past, my obvious failure to appear attractive in the eyes of my husband, and the possibility that at any time the sailor's confession would destroy the small hope I had for a future.

One of the young women who must have been waiting outside the bedchamber door for my call, arrived promptly with a breakfast tray before I could ring. She seemed to be concealing, though badly, some excitement that made her large dark eyes glitter and her mouth twitch, with dimples waiting to flash in easy laughter. I hoped I might borrow her warm good humor.

"Good morning. You are Darielle, aren't you? Isn't it a beautiful day?"

"Yes, madame." She curtseyed. "A beautiful day." She was still stifling a giggle, so it could not be simply the beauty of the day that produced such good humor. I looked at the tray and was touched by the effort that had gone into making it especially welcoming and delicious-looking. There was a large single flower the color of blood—no! the color of a scarlet bird—whose stamen was long and obtrusive. The flower had been placed so artlessly that it seemed a delightful afterthought.

The food itself was appetizingly prepared. Instead of tea or chocolate there was coffee in the silver pot, and beside the silver knife were two fruits that I did not recognize: a green-skinned globe with pink, seeded flesh, and a small fruit with a sharp, but not unappealing flavor. There was also a miniature round loaf of freshly baked white bread. No butter had been provided, but Mama had never served it with bread either. She claimed that bread should be fresh enough to eat without such "disguise."

"What is the news?" I asked, breaking bites of the warm bread and sipping the coffee, which was very strong and as thick as Turkish coffee, although Darielle pointed out that it came from New Orleans in the French sector of the North Continent. New Orleans, I knew, was still held back from that recent purchase of Louisiana and Mississippi River lands by the president of the United States. There was much commerce between France and her young protégé, due to their common dislike of Britain; and trade in these islands remained as brisk as ever, despite British control.

"Oh, madame! What excitement!"

I wanted to know if my husband had set out to capture the missing sailor, but without looking up, I said more calmly than I felt, "They have caught the man they were searching for yesterday?"

Darielle was surprised. "No, madame. Not so. It is only that Le Maréchal was seen in Port Fleur last night, and he escaped." She watched me, obviously gauging whether I would be friend or foe in the matter of the rebel leader.

I smiled. "He must have friends along the leeward coast."

"Indeed, yes. He is a hero, madame. Even the governor admires him. Tirsa says the governor will one day give over British power to—" She clapped her hand over her mouth as discretion came too late. I was not interested in Le Maréchal at the moment, except in regard to the housekeeper's sympathies. It did not seem particularly wise of Ian Douglas to keep in his employ a woman whose allegiance was to his enemies. However, I would have to break my horrible habit of suspecting everyone about me. It was the governor's concern, after all, and he must have at least some knowledge of her views.

"I suppose the colonel is out on the search," I said casually.

"He was," Darielle nodded, adding in dejection, "it is a great pity, madame. They would understand each other. We say that often."

I had it on the tip of my tongue to ask who "they" might be. But I caught myself. If I were ever to become a decent, straightforward human being, I had best not go about betraying people for their casual remarks. Nevertheless, my old training made me acutely aware of all the nuances in Ian Douglas's household. I wondered if he had any conception of the potential disloyalty among his servants. And I thought myself a very good judge of traitors, having been one myself.

I was still trying to broach the subject of my husband's whereabouts when Darielle answered my unspoken question as she removed my tray.

"When it is convenient to you, madame, His Excellency wonders if you will favor him with a few minutes of your time this morning."

How absurdly formal! I would have liked to believe

the formality was accidental, a part of his nature, but I feared that for some reason I could not guess, the form in which he put the request was deliberate and sardonic. Why?

"I will dress at once. I slept too long. I should never have. . . . Please have him informed that I will be ready in ten minutes."

The girl looked astonished. Perhaps she was used to the French ladies who, according to Mama, had taken hours to complete their toilettes. But she took my tray from the room and hurried back with Pepine and the third girl to aid me in the fantastic act of dressing in ten minutes. Fortunately, I had begun to dress without aid and was nearly ready by the time they returned, for I had noted that the more assistance I received, the slower I managed to be. They helped me with my hair, and I asked then, taking up an East Indian shawl which I certainly would not need in this climate, "Where am I to meet His Excellency?"

Pepine and Darielle exchanged glances, and Pepine said, "But—here. That is to say, in your sitting room, madame. His Excellency did not imagine you would be ready so quickly." Her tone suggested that my haste was somehow unladylike, but I ignored this implication and asked Darielle to lead the way to my husband. Privately, I considered this formality absurd. I liked to think that I was very much a product of the French Revolution and of the new century.

As I passed a console mirror that gleamed in the daylight, I saw a reflection of my figure clad in lilac muslin and walking too rapidly for proper grace and elegance. I reduced my speed and concentrated on presenting the cool, sophisticated façade my husband evidently preferred. Catching a glimpse of Pepine behind me in the hall, it occurred to me suddenly that Ian

Douglas's formality and indifference had a natural explanation. He possessed a mistress whose manifold attractions relegated mine to the dust. I understood the situation but resented it. Or was I envious? Surely not! The man was selfish and arrogant, possibly brutal in action and certainly brutal in speech. But I had made my bargain and would carry it out.

Darielle led me to a small bookroom on the ground floor, which also appeared to be the governor's office. It was only reached through the pink-and-gold salon, where government officials no doubt waited before being received in private. Long windows in the sheer west face of the building overlooked the outer bay as did my own suite. The sun glittered blindingly upon the waters.

The governor was at his desk, a large, cluttered, cheap piece of furniture that was obviously utilitarian. I was impressed again, almost in spite of myself, that Colonel Ian Douglas was no stuffed uniform, no figurehead. He cared about his work and meant to make his governorship a success. These were qualities I admired. I almost wished I did not admire them so much. In view of our chilly relationship, I would almost have preferred to believe he spent his hours wenching.

He did not notice me at once; he was bent over a map of the island. Then, raising his head and seeing me, he looked so surprised that I wanted to laugh. I did not, however. I remained demurely before him and murmured, "I was told you wished to speak to me, sir."

"I did, but in your rooms, madame. You needn't have come down here. What can I say, except—"

"Good morning would be an excellent start."

I had shaken him. Good! He had some feelings. He

had appeared quite human for a moment or two, but he quickly reverted to the cocksure fellow with the easy sarcasm.

"Of course. And you had a good night, my dear Madeline? Anyone can see that you had. You are in extraordinary looks today. What a shame to waste them upon a mere husband!" He laughed, and while I stared, Darielle giggled with him, although I doubted that she understood him.

"You are too kind, my dear Ian." I put every ounce of irony I possessed into the compliment. "But now that I am here, you may as well make the most of it. You did want to speak to me, or so I was given to understand."

"You act as if my request were some kind of command." All his hackles were raised, but behind the prickly exterior I felt a strongly sensual interest which matched my own awareness of his attractions. I was delighted and a little nervous at the prospect that we at least shared one emotion. I could see that it was his pride—or perhaps the memory of a long-ago rejection by another female—which made him so wary.

"Wasn't it a command?" I teased him. "And it succeeded. I am here."

He glowered at me suspiciously. There was a tense little bond between us. I was certain we were both aware of it. He seemed almost on the verge of seizing me, whether to shake me or kiss me, I had no notion. I was not averse to the idea, in either case, for it argued a strong feeling. Then he recovered himself, and gave Darielle a brief look. It seemed to be sufficient; she left us alone. I went over and pulled a chair toward his desk, forestalling his own intention. He was annoyed, but contented himself by pushing my chair closer with me in it.

"How are you finding St. Sebastien?"

"Very pleasant, from what I have seen so far." I felt like remarking on his uncharacteristic reluctance to bring up whatever troubled him, but I was absolutely determined to force him to work at his inquisitor's role. He must know about the message from Agnes Mabberly and intend that I should suffer first, before he got to the point of an accusation.

"Happy to hear you say so. Now, my dear girl, I'd like to hear what you know of your cousin's habits."

"His habits! George?" Good heavens! What had this to do with anything?

"I mean, is he in the hands of moneylenders? Does he play for high stakes? Has he any enemies that you are aware of?"

"But you would know that better than I. He has been in the service a few years now. He worships you. Or in any case, he regards your word as law." I could not imagine what this was about. George in a money-lender's hands? But he would have told me, surely. I might have helped in some way. I had often given him money in our youth.

My husband focused on me with a sudden, penetrating look. It reminded me of a prosecutor's stare, and though I tried not to betray its powerful effect, I was shaken by the recollection that this man could order me hanged for my "crimes against the State."

"Then perhaps you can tell me why that sailor on the *Maud Vester* tried to murder him?"

Had my face colored slightly with relief? I kept my fingers in my lap, caught in the threads of my shawl, and hoped they did not shake. "Is that what Captain Hollin told you?"

Was he looking at my hands? No. His gaze shifted from me to the window behind me, as though his thoughts were leagues away. But I still suspected he was as sharp as a Bow Street Runner.

"Hollin was vague about the entire affair. Can you tell me what happened, how the fellow failed? Dropped a case of the rifles I was expecting. So much I know. But until Adare returns from the search, I've no notion what is at the root of all this business."

I explained to him what I had seen, adding with perfect honesty that George had said "the fellow barely missed me" or words to that effect.

"I assumed he meant that it was an accident," I said. "George can tell you better than I what his thoughts and suspicions were."

"And that is all you have to say?" As my head snapped up with indignation that concealed my fear, he put up one hand to ward off an outburst from me. "I expressed that badly. You are right, of course. I had best put the questions to Captain Adare." He shuffled the map under one hand.

I thought, *He is nervous. This excessively confident man is nervous.*

I was not so conceited as to imagine I might be the cause, but it was odd, all the same. This entire talk had been strange. Was it only in order to question me about my cousin that he had demanded to see me this morning? What an impossible man! And yet, by his small weaknesses, he endeared himself to me.

"Is that all, my dear Ian?"

He hesitated, continuing to study the map, which looked to me like masses of green with a peculiar, deep-brown circle with ragged edges, like dried blood, near the eastern center section of the island. He dismissed me without raising his eyes from the map.

"That is all. Incidentally, British rule was definitely aided last night. Thank you."

"A pleasure." I smiled and started out. As I passed him, he reached for my hand. Our fingers barely brushed before he drew away, stiffening slightly, and turned back to his desk. For a moment he had almost revealed a liking for me.

I went out through the salon where a soldier and two men in wide-brimmed planter's hats and sans-culotte trousers waited. Although I felt that I had managed my part of the little scene with my husband discreetly, I was not certain how much he knew, or how much Agnes Mabberly had confided to him. What if he were merely playing a game with me and knew more than he had hinted?

I must see Agnes Mabberly. I would live on a knife's edge until I discovered what she had learned from my would-be assassin, what she intended to tell my husband, or what—for a price—she intended not to tell him.

I saw Tirsa supervising the removal of flower decorations from the dining salon. I said good morning. The housekeeper smiled slightly, inclined her head, and repeated my brief greeting before hurrying her workingmen on about their business. I did not know she was still watching me as I walked to the portico, and I was a little shaken by her sharp, authoritative call to me.

"Madame Douglas! You are leaving Government House? You will require your maid and the carriage."

I started to object. I had not considered this problem. The servants who accompanied me would gossip, but I knew that a lady alone in Port Fleur, and the governor's lady at that, would be even more shocking than my occasional visits alone to a mercer's shop in London, had made me. These trips had caused enough scandal so that mothers of well-bred young ladies often refused to allow me in their houses. I could not allow myself to be ostracized here.

"Yes, of course," I said. "Darielle will come. I had best order the carriage brought around."

"I had best order it," Tirsa corrected me in a tone very like a schoolmistress'.

And thus, with pomp and ceremony, I was to start on my secret visit, in full view of two servants and every busybody in Port Fleur. During the short trip around the bay and into town I would have to exercise my ingenuity in trying to discover a way of evading them all. It was not easy, but at last I found a method that would give me my chance to be completely alone in the town for a brief interval. There was the matter of my own safety, but I was not afraid for that. I had spent most of my life dealing in intrigue.

I went up to my bedchamber and found Pepine and the other maid smoothing my bed with its elaborate green counterpane. While they left me alone briefly I took down several bonnets. The charming lilac taffeta matched my gown but would be far too noticeable. Instead, I decided upon a dark-brown one, unflattering but practical in the rain. It also concealed my face, which was of more moment now. I changed to an old shawl, very large, which certainly subdued my lilac gown. I tied my bonnet strings, wound the shawl around me, picked up my reticule, and started down to the portico where Darielle and Shimbé were awaiting me in the open carriage.

# 8

I was perfectly aware that the carriage itself marked
me as the wife of the governor, but I hoped I might
evade this problem when I left the vehicle in the town
long enough to visit Mrs. Mabberly. We drove along
the dusty road that ringed the harbor, descending pre-
cipitously as we reached the hibiscus-covered huts on
the edge of ' )wn. There was a new ship in the harbor,
a nondescript barkentine whose longboats were already bobbing empty along the quai. The man who
stood watch looked suspiciously like a pirate.

"I've never seen a pirate ship," I remarked to Darielle, "but that man's as near to a cutthroat as I'd care
to meet."

"It is a slave ship in from West Africa, ma'am. They
touched at New Orleans, and the cargo not sold there
is to be put on the auction block here at noon today.
You may see the crowd passing the Quai des Fleurs.
The block is beyond, in the *carrefour*—that is, the
square—at the north end of the street. Most of them
will be bought for the cane brakes, far inland. There
will be no house servants in that lot." She eyed the
whole business with detachment.

Our carriage and patient mare were soon caught up
in the excitement on the quais and were forced to
move more slowly than I myself could walk. Most of

the buyers hurrying to the auction must be planters or their overseers, judging by their big palmetto hats and homespun clothing that suited the hot, moist local weather, but others in that crowd must be hurrying there out of morbid curiosity, and I was distressed to see many children among them.

"Set me down here beside the *savane* and I will look into some mercers' shops to see what goods the local ladies are buying," I said.

Shimbé pulled up at the dusty park, and this time I waited until he could help me down. Darielle insisted on going with me, but I had expected that. There was one advantage to the grim affair going on across the town: none of the townspeople paid much heed to me. The traffic was all to the north, beyond the little shops in the center of Port Fleur. I started up one square and into the narrow, cobbled street parallel to the waterfront. There were deep gulleys on either side of the street where sewage ran, or rather was clogged in foul heaps where the repulsive but apparently useful vultures drifted down and set to work disposing of it. In order to reach a candlemaker's shop with a deep, overhanging wooden roof as a protection against the sun, Darielle and I had to step over quantities of refuse, disturbing a huge winged creature with a curved, pendulous beak, an image out of a nightmare. He very nearly disputed the passage with me.

The smells were worse than in a London slum, but looking around, I noticed that these odors did not seem to trouble the citizens of Port Fleur, and I suspected that I too would in time grow used to them.

I went into the dark, musty little candlemaker's shop. There were no other patrons, and the merchandise appeared dusty and faded. This situation would not suit my plans. I made a pretense of examining the

candles, including the molds which the French shopkeeper assured me would be in use on the morrow and
would be of interest to a lady "who, naturally, did not
make her own candles."

After an examination of the candles—tallow dipped
to form odd shapes and sizes, and wax tapers that
tilted a little after long exposure to the local heat—I
felt I had persuaded Darielle of my casual intentions. I
purchased two tapers less tipsy than the others, and
went out onto the narrow walkway on the shop side of
the great, running gutter.

A mercer's shop further along the street proved
more rewarding for my purpose. It was crowded with
shelves full of materials: rare cottons with appropri-
ately high prices, and gauzes for evening wear, which
looked a trifle shopworn. The black shopkeeper
brought out lengths of Lyons silks as well.

"Very popular at the French court, madame. The
Emperor's favorite, we are told."

I had heard the rumors that Napoleon wished to
promote the Lyons silk industry, but I knew also that,
like most males, he could not persuade his wife. She
persisted in ordering muslins and cottons, often smuggled into France from British possessions. And of
course, in this Caribbean climate heavy silk was less
practical than Indiennes and muslin.

Across the room, which smelled of curious Oriental
incense and sweat from used gowns for sale, I saw great
bins of sea shells.

"For buttons, madame. For buttons and for decorat-
ing baskets and perhaps shoes, and casquettes for ladies' jewels. For many things."

I pretended a fascination with the shells, and began
to make a fuss over some small ones with pink pearl
interiors. There must be thousands of them, I thought;

it would take many minutes, perhaps hours to sort them out for particular size and color. Good! This was the chance I had hoped for.

I made a pretense of fingering the shells and then, as Darielle and the shopkeeper watched me, I looked up as if I had suddenly been struck by a marvelous idea.

"Darielle! Will you oblige me? I'm persuaded you have excellent taste and a good eye for color."

Pleased and smiling, she came over and peered into the bin. She clapped her hands.

"Yes, madame. They are so pretty. See? That one. And this with the blue and pink and silver. I have seen skies in the east at sunset that looked so."

"I knew I could trust you, Darielle. I would very much like to buy these. About a hundred. Of exactly the same color, and as nearly of a size as possible. Meanwhile, I will look into the shops from here to the *carrefour* where the other streets cross. When I return you will have completed the selection."

"Oh, but màdame—"

"You are so skillful. You will help me enormously. A few minutes only. You understand?"

The poor girl was still confused when I waved to her and left the shop. I hurried along under the wooden awnings, aided by the press of citizens and slaves pushing in the direction I wished to go, for the auction block was beyond the inn where I had seen Agnes Mabberly the day before. I knew I could reach the inn within two or three minutes.

Several men were seated around a little table at the front of the inn, in imitation of the tables outside cafés in Venice and Paris, but luckily no one paid much attention to me. I went past them into the surprisingly cool interior where I faced a blast of rum-scented air. I had walked into the taproom.

I rapped on the roughened board surface and called, "Tapster!"

A small man with a rodent's sharp, clever little face and an ingratiating smile that showed an inordinate amount of teeth, popped out from the passage, as black as night behind the tapster's bar.

"Madame called me?"

"I am looking for Mrs. Mabberly. Can you tell me where I may find her?"

His jaw dropped. "Madame is a—a friend to Agnes?"

"We met on shipboard. We voyaged to St. Sebastien on the *Maud Vester*." A sudden daring impulse made me add, "The governor's lady was aboard. She suffered from seasickness."

"Aye," the little man began confidentially. "So do they all. You may depend on it, madame, that wretched cargo they are offering on the block today would be in far better condition if they had not suffered so violently from the seasickness."

"I have no doubt of it. Where may I find Mrs. Mabberly?"

"Gone into the Mourne district to visit some wounded wretch that her girls came to know on shipboard. A sailor, I believe. Had some business with the rebels, bringing them money or something, and the governor's soldiers shot him. He escaped and made his way to the Mourne Swamp where Agnes's girl was entertaining the rebel leader, this—"

"Le Maréchal," I said. "But I believe that is supposed to be a secret. You had better forget you heard the name." So this sailor had delivered money to the rebels? Small wonder! As Luc Monceau's agent, he might very well be furnishing the rebels with money or weapons to defeat the British. The sailor's attempt to kill me had probably been only the lesser part of his assignment from Monceau.

The little man glanced back into the darkness. "I want no trouble with the rebels, you understand, ma'am."

"Yes, yes, but how do I reach Mrs. Mabberly?"

"There is an alley. Follow that to the road which crosses the copse. They call it a swamp, but it's no space at all to one that's known the moors of the West Riding. You'll doubtless see her ahead of you on the road, if you hurry."

I took leave to doubt that a swamp on St. Sebastien was any less fearful than the Yorkshire moors, but then, I had never been lost on the infamous moors. I thanked him, and as he stood aside for me to pass—careful that his body touched mine as I did so—I loosened the strings of my reticule, took out some silver and coppers, and dropped them into his palm. He backed up to count the coins.

"Ah! English. Good. Many prefer the French coinage, now that Bonaparte has rid us of that useless Revolutionary paper, but for me—give me a good, sound guinea any day."

"Not today, however," I said firmly, as I went on through that dark, musty passage.

I heard his sniggering laughter behind me, but by this time I was nearly at the back door. I passed a flight of stairs which I assumed must lead up to the quarters occupied by Mrs. Mabberly's girls. The stairs, surprisingly, were carpeted. In all likelihood, the quarters in which Agnes and the two girls entertained the men of St. Sebastien—including my husband?—

were much grander than the commonplace taproom belowstairs.

Out in the narrow alley which also served as a street at the rear of the inn, I found as much activity as on the main street. However, huge bushes of flowers protected or concealed the ramshackle backs of the buildings, and although sewage was emptied here too, the smells were less offensive. But it was uncomfortable walking here, because I lacked the protection of my husband's identy; I was simply another female who might be English or French, and my virtue or lack of it was a matter of conjecture. I sensed this as I moved rapidly in the direction of a distant clump of trees. Their branches were so closely interwoven that I could not guess whether they were a wild profusion of flowering bushes, or the beginnings of the Mourne Swamp.

I hurried my steps, aware that more than one of the men I had seen striding toward the auction block now took an unnerving interest in me as the only female to be seen in this long, winding alley. I had not thought I would be relieved to see the beginnings of the little tapster's "copse," but so it was. The alley had wound upward for several minutes, and now turned north. Great masses of purple blossoms lined the path, growing in such luxuriance that they joined over my head to mingle with lianas dangling and twisting like so many serpents. Bushes of the commonplace red hibiscus appeared, fresh and cheerful, among the more spectacular blooms, and small, scarcely noticeable yellow flowers gave off an almost suffocating perfume.

I had not yet spied Agnes Mabberly, and I began to hurry. After a minute or two I glanced over my shoulder. A powerful-looking black field worker, dressed in breeches and a wide-brimmed palmetto hat, was stalk-

ing along behind me. I could not remember whether
he had been among the crowd in the street. Perhaps he
was merely on his way across the Mourne Swamp; I
did not know what lay beyond the place where Mrs.
Mabberly was looking after the traitorous English
sailor. As I slowed my pace, pretending to look over
into a trickling stream which paralled the path, I
noted with enormous relief that my pursuer strode on,
passing me without a glance, and was soon lost to my
sight around a twist and turn in the path.

Huge, many-forked tree roots set up a natural barrier and made it even more difficult for me to see
Agnes Mabberly ahead of me, if, indeed, she was on
the road. And I was beginning to doubt that ingratiating tapster. The barrier to the path provided by the
huge trunk of that outlandish tree gave me an idea.
The tree only half concealed a low, hilly region on my
left, a hillock of about a man's height. If I made my
way through the slimy underbrush to the top of that
little knoll, I might get a better view of what lay
ahead on this trail. I lifted my skirts, managing, for
the most part, to protect them with my shawl, and
stepped carefully through the underbrush. As I found
myself above the ground where I had stood, I made
out the trail ahead and saw something which confirmed me in my suspicion of danger.

The man in the palmetto hat was standing in the
shadow of a deep thicket beyond the sluggish stream.
He faced the direction in which I should appear in
another minute, and I was convinced that he waited
for me. Yet, I still couldn't imagine why he hadn't attacked or even killed me when he passed me a few
minutes earlier. I backed down the slope a few steps to
prevent my silhouette from becoming a target, for my

position was only partially concealed by the gigantic ferns and other vegetation.

Suddenly, in moving, I saw a small footpath cutting westward just below the knoll on which I stood. My pursuer waited a few steps beyond this fork in the trail. It seemed to me that this explained what he was up to. He had stationed himself to see which fork of the trail I took. And if I took the wrong one . . . ?

I stepped closer to the edge, immediately above the footpath, and espied a hut further west, a matter of scarcely more than a minute's walk. The hut appeared to be one large room with a small veranda under an overhanging roof. The stillness of the swamp enabled me to hear voices coming from inside, and I was sure one of them was Agnes Mabberly's.

I moved carefully down the slope to the back of the hut, listening as I might have listened in the old days when I worked for Luc Monceau—by force of habit, one might say.

Mrs. Mabberly's voice was not quite the pleasant, low-pitched one I recalled from our friendly conversations on the *Maud Vester*. But then, I had never heard her conduct business.

"You may take it or you may leave it, but I'll not have my girls put to danger for your precious cause, no matter how saintly your leader is. Do I make myself clear?"

"Abundantly, ma'am, abundantly," said a smooth male voice that sounded vaguely familiar. "One could not mistake your—ah—musical tones. Every word is graved upon my heart."

Lieutenant Felipe. My husband's trusted officer. This man was a part of the islanders' rebellion. If he saw me here now, he would realize that my knowledge of his identity as a rebel offered an enormous threat to

his career and to his leader, Le Maréchal. I stopped
and considered my next move. My shoes were sinking
into the muck of dead foliage brought down by a recent rainfall, and I shifted them, feeling the nasty pull
of mud beneath my feet.

"I sent my girl to oblige your precious leader,"
Agnes Mabberly said sharply. "The fact that she was
here when that wounded sailor stumbled in upon her
and Le Maréchal is of no interest to her. She will not
talk."

"My dear Mrs. Mabberly, the sailor was a friend to
the rebels. He brought the means for purchasing ammunition, as your young lady is very much aware.
Why should we let him die? And your girl merely wit-
nessed his arrival. Why do you think Le Maréchal
would harm her? Unless, of course, you were indiscreet
about his presence here? Come. Examine the fellow
yourself. We had no reason to kill him. He was shot
by the English soldiers, not by us."

I caught my breath. Was the murderous sailor still
alive, and perhaps able to talk? Did the treacherous
Lieutenant Felipe know my secret? Had the sailor
talked to him or to others among Le Maréchal's men?

"Now, I have my duties," Lieutenant Felipe went
on suddenly. "The noble Colonel Douglas is expecting
me to complete the search. I need not repeat, I hope,
what will happen to you if anything is said of the leader's presence here last night."

I leaped back, feeling the sinister power of that
threat, and managed to conceal myself within the
branches of gigantic ferns and a flowering tree whose
yellow blossoms spread wide enough to hide half a
dozen eavesdroppers. As I had guessed, the man who
came out of the hut was my husband's "loyal" Lieutenant Felipe, tall, lithe, with his serpentlike grace. I

did not move until he had gone around the bluff where I hoped he would set off along the main trail into town.

As I stepped onto the solid, well-tamped ground under the overhanging roof, Agnes Mabberly opened the door. She still looked shaken and angry after her conversation with Lieutenant Felipe, and my unexpected appearance was obviously unwelcome.

"You! How did you find me here?" She started to step outside, closing the door behind her, and I knew she wanted to hide the sailor. It was an instinctive gesture, because she must have known I would answer her letter some time.

"Your note last night gave me a hint of where I would find you." I took a deep breath, afraid to ask her the most important question. Afraid not to. "I assume that last night you gave my husband the information you had previously written to me."

Agnes Mabberly looked older, worn and tired, which was not surprising in view of the danger she had encountered out here in Mourne Swamp. The fact that she was known to have information about one of Le Maréchal's hiding places would be enough to terrify her. She smiled, but with a bitter edge.

"You think so? Then you did not tell the governor yourself? I would have thought you might. There is something very odd about your relationship with that sailor, Mrs. Douglas."

"Because he wanted to kill me? I am English. He is working for the French. Isn't that enough?" I had not intended to sound so sharp. A questioning, perplexed tone would have been less suspicious.

"He confessed he had two missions here. One is not your concern. But the other was to murder you."

"I wondered when I read your note last night. I suppose a man might attempt to murder Colonel Douglas's betrothed. There are many reasons why such an act might seem politically helpful. To someone devoted to the local rebel leader, for instance."

Agnes Mabberly started at my mention of Le Maréchal. She pressed her body against the door. I did not want to worry her or to make trouble for her; I remembered our friendship on the *Maud Vester*. But I put her aside gently, yet as firmly as I could, and pushed the door open.

The sailor, Peter Phipps, was lying on a pile of filthy, bloodstained rags on a cot of some kind. Unshaven and badly scratched by his flight through the jungle, he appeared to be unconscious. But he was breathing stertorously. I had a single moment of shocking self-awareness: I had hoped to see him dead.

Well, then, it was not to be. I would not escape the harm of this man's knowledge. But although I knew it would be easy enough to kill him—a small matter of smothering him, perhaps—I thanked God that Luc Monceau's calm, sallow, keen-eyed face flashed suddenly across my brain, and I asked myself if I wanted to be as ruthless as he. I had deserted Monceau partly because I could not condone murder. Nor would I condone it in myself.

"Shouldn't the fellow have a surgeon?" I asked Agnes, who studied me almost as if she could read my thoughts.

"We dare not. He may talk and tell the authorities it was Le Maréchal's pistol that caused the wound. A misunderstanding, as it was explained to me. The leader thought he was being attacked and shot at him."

I noted the discrepancy between her story and the

account she had given me in her note. I supposed that fear had impelled her to tell me the truth.

"Just so," María-Vega said from outside the hut. "But the governor's men must not know about Le Maréchal."

"For the governor's sake as well. It would be disastrous to his wife if the leader were captured," Agnes reminded me.

"I understand. But what are we to do?" I said. In a sense I agreed with her about Le Maréchal. My husband might be an excellent administrator, and I suspected that he was, but he and his government were new on St. Sebastien, and alien to the population of the island. The capture of Le Maréchal would destroy any hope Ian Douglas might have of consolidating a just and honest rule here. Lieutenant Felipe's treachery, however, was of much more immediate concern.

Agnes moved to the cot where the wounded man had begun to twitch and groan.

"Water . . ." He opened his eyes and stared, unblinking, across the room at me. I wondered if he really saw me at all. Then he muttered, directly to me, "Needn't think you'll escape. He said—if I fail—I gave letters . . . other—"

"Other?" I could hardly get the word out. I felt weak, stupefied by this new hint of danger.

"Other agent. Take my place now. You'll not escape."

Agnes lifted a rum mug of fresh water to the man's lips. He drank greedily, all the while staring at me over the rim of the mug.

Agnes followed his glance, then gave me a brisk nod toward the door. "Go now, please. He is talking nonsense. You will be quite safe while he is in this condition."

"What do you mean—safe!" Did she know a great deal more than she pretended?

"He wanted to kill you. You can see he is quite helpless now. You have nothing to worry about. If he recovers . . . well, we must deal with that when it happens. There are those who would like to see him remain alive. He came to St. Sebastien to help the rebels. But do not mention this, if you value our lives, yours and mine."

"I understand." I wondered if she had heard his mumbling words well enough to comprehend them. The mention of letters was a mystery to me, but now I knew there would be other agents, if he failed. Luc Monceau never did things by halves. I hesitated, and in that brief, silent space of time, we heard a footstep on the wooden plank over the mud at the doorway, then Lieutenant Felipe's voice.

"Mrs. Mabberly, am I wrong, or do you have an unexpected visitor?"

# 9

I felt trapped. Lieutenant Felipe easily might murder me if he thought I had heard him admit his connection with the rebel leader. Unless, of course, he had learned my own secret from the wounded sailor. A single look around the hut told me there was no way out of the place. There was nothing for it but to brave out a meeting with the lieutenant. The fact that I myself had once been a traitor did not, however, make me appreciate the lieutenant's treachery against my husband.

At least I had a moment to compose myself before Lieutenant Felipe pushed the door wide open. He was smiling as he greeted the flustered Agnes Mabberly, but when he appeared to see me for the first time, and his narrow eyes did not even blink, I was certain he had known all along that he would find me here.

"Good afternoon, Lieutenant," I hailed him before he could speak. "You are fast becoming my heroic rescuer. First at the quai yesterday, and now in the midst of this horrid jungle."

This time his heavy eyelids did flicker. I knew I had taken him aback. But he recovered rapidly, with a graceful bow. "How am I to rescue Madame? Anything, including a march over hot coals, will be my pleasure, I assure you."

"You are too gallant, Lieutenant. I shall not ask you to go so far. Only to accompany me to my carriage, which I was thoughtless enough to leave somewhere near the *savane* on the Quai des Fleurs."

He said nothing about the wounded man. It was as though the man did not exist. I suspected he was waiting for me to reveal some knowledge of the sailor, so instead I repeated, "Truly, Lieutenant, I would appreciate your escort."

Agnes Mabberly was so nervous that I thought he would notice, but to her evident astonishment he offered his arm to me. "You—you came back. Why did you come back?" she stammered then.

He had not asked what I was doing here, and he lied breezily now. "Really, do you know, I have no notion. It might as well have been for the privilege of escorting Madame Douglas back to her carriage. One likes to give precedence where it is due." His sarcasm was rather obvious for a man of his smooth tongue, but he had been thrown off his stride. "Whatever the reason, it has flown away now." He gave me a melting smile. "How fortunate for me that I should find Madame here! The last place in St. Sebastien that one would expect to find the governor's wife. Perhaps she has been conducting my search for me? We are all anxious to locate any of the rebel leader's men."

I was equally sparkling in my insincerity. "It is a coincidence that you have come to this place. I was curious to see the sailor who caused the dangerous accident yesterday. Why anyone should attempt to kill my poor Cousin George, I cannot imagine, and if this fellow is the one responsible, he must have a reason."

He could not hide his surprise at my bringing up the identity of the wounded man. As for me, I was anxious to keep the lieutenant off the subject of Le

Maréchal, which would be a good deal more dangerous to Agnes and to me. I could imagine how he had
hoped to taunt me with veiled comments about the
jungle visit, on our way back to the town. My bland
confession had thwarted that attempt, for he must
know I had recognized this wounded man.

"So that's the rogue!" he pretended to see the dazed
and staring sailor for the first time. "Well, we must
bring him in. What seems to ail him, madame?"

He turned to Agnes, who said hurriedly, "The fever
now, I think. He was badly cut up in the swamp. I
explained to Mrs. Douglas that we had not been certain of his identity, although María-Vega thought she
had seen him on the *Maud Vester*. Mrs. Douglas felt
that since we were by no means certain of his deliberate guilt, she had best question him before we informed the governor. But—"

"But," I interrupted, waving aside the matter as of
no consequence, "we could discover nothing. The man
is unconscious. And I, for one, believe it has all been
much ado about nothing. I shall tell the governor so."

"Perhaps," cut in Lieutenant Felipe, "for the sake
of this unfortunate rogue, it would be humane of us
not to mention the matter to the governor until the
man is in better case to be moved."

If the lieutenant guessed I knew his connection with
Le Maréchal, I would not be likely to leave here alive,
but his casual request enormously relieved me. I
agreed not to mention the sailor to my husband. As if
I wanted to! And the lieutenant obligingly helped me
over the sill and onto the path. I caught Agnes Mabberly's quickly rolled eyes, expressive of her equal relief, and I am sure my brief glance conveyed my
shared feelings. Lieutenant Felipe did not look back. I
wondered if it was because he was so sure of himself.

We passed through the glade where the overhanging foliage was so thick that we felt the deadly, stifling heat of the sun without seeing it overhead.

"There is a shorter path," the lieutenant suggested as we were nearing the stream which ran beside the main trail.

"I am sure the usual path is satisfactory. I came this way before."

"Of course, as you choose." But he had obviously wished me to take some mysterious short path which would, perhaps, make it easier to dispose of me if the need arose.

I looked about quickly to see if the native man who had followed me was still waiting near the junction of the trail and the path, but no one was in sight.

"Now, I wonder whom—or what—you are searching for in that underbrush, madame."

His light, almost gentle voice was far more sinister than an obvious accusation would have been. But I refused to let him guess how he had alarmed me. I pretended to take his suggestion literally and said in a puzzled voice, "There was a man here earlier, a worker from the cane fields, I think. He passed me on the trail and then I saw him again over in that thicket." I did not doubt that he was one of Felipe's sentinels.

His disappointment amused me. Did he hope to catch me in some absurd and childish mistake? All the same, it was the small, foolish things that betrayed us, my father had once warned me. To protect myself further, I said casually, "How well traveled this trail is! One would imagine it to be the leading boulevard of the island." I had seen no one ahead of us, but hoped he would not be sure the trail was empty.

He glanced ahead, then smiled. He did not even

trouble to look behind us. His fingers fastened upon my arm.

"Here. You nearly trod upon a snake."

I jumped, and found myself much too close to that repulsive, weed-choked stream which, I had no doubt, was crawling with vermin, spiders, and poisonous reptiles. I was furious with myself for having let him frighten me, but it was too late to regret my silly cowardice.

"Ah, you are right. The ground is firmer here," he said.

I attempted to move back onto the right side of the trail, for it now sloped downward and I was picking my way through the soggy debris of the swamp, but his body prevented me. He was determined that I should approach the unpleasant, and perhaps even deadly stream below.

"Heavens!" I said, laughing at the plain absurdity of his statement. "You will have me tumbling into the stream!" He looked at me, frowning for the first time. I was pleased that I obviously puzzled him. "What endless complications that would cause my poor husband, Lieutenant!"

Pretending to play my game of danger, he asked, "But how would your husband know that you had taken this very odd trail, madame?"

Airily, I lied. "My tiresome maid. I have already found that one cannot keep secrets where she is involved. Silly creature! She insisted there was a quicker way to that hut, but I did not wish her to accompany me—such gossips as maids usually are! Still, the loyal soul may have hung about just to walk back with me. She considers it highly improper for a lady to go about St. Sebastian without an entourage."

"And so it is!" He said this so harshly that he might have been an overbearing husband, but at least he no longer showed symptoms of letting me fall into that horrid stream.

I began to recall certain landmarks and was relieved to note that we had reached the outskirts of Port Fleur. I released myself from the lieutenant's custody, explaining that if I had not met Darielle near the trail to Mourne Swamp, we were to meet at the mercer's shop. He insisted on escorting me there. I was almost afraid to meet the girl, remembering that an hour had passed since I had assured her I would only be gone a few minutes. However, there was nothing for it but to enter the mercer's shop with Lieutenant Felipe close behind me, while I prepared an elaborate speech explaining that I had been so enraptured by the local flora and fauna in a garden beyond the *carrefour*, that I could not tear myself away.

Darielle stood at the long counter, a little separated from several other shoppers whom the mercer waited upon while exchanging the day's gossip. As I came in, she cried out anxiously, "Ma'am! I am so sorry. It cannot be helped. We have done our very best."

Concerned at her anguish, I hurried over. Spread upon the counter was what appeared to be an endless collection of small, dainty shells of almost an exact size.

Darielle murmured in that scared voice, "We have tried and tried, but we can only find eighty-nine. And you wished one hundred."

Very much ashamed of myself for having put her through this boring business, I said quickly, "It doesn't matter, Darielle. I appreciate what you have found. Let us pay the man and be done. I daresay they will be wondering about us at Government House."

"I did not mean to take so long," she protested, and then sucked in her breath abruptly at sight of Lieutenant Felipe.

I looked at him. "You have been most kind, Lieutenant. I must remember to tell my husband how obliging you were."

"Madame is very good." I had turned away, but something in his voice put me on my guard. "Very good, and with such a fine regard for the truth." I stiffened, and he held up one finger in playful remonstrance. "But perhaps this is not the servant who so obligingly waited for you at the mouth of our Mourne Swamp."

"Not at all," I said, trying to match the smoothness of his sharp-edged taunt. I thought quickly of the first similar name that came to my mind. "You misunderstood me. Mirella was the girl. She must have returned to the carriage. . . . I shall not need you now. Again, my thanks." I held out my hand, and he was forced to bend over it. "Come, Darielle," I went on. "Shall we choose some lengths of that beautiful silk? Even though it is French, I am persuaded we may find some use for it." Lieutenant Felipe seemed uncertain, half inclined to remain even yet, so I added, "And that figured muslin! Utterly delicious. From the Orient, I presume."

Seeing that there was nothing for it but to give up, the lieutenant stalked out, too angry to exhibit his usual grace. I exhaled in enormous relief, and joined Darielle at the counter. I found myself almost hysterically glad to have gotten rid of him, if only for the moment. When he became certain of what I knew about the wounding of the sailor, and the presence of

Le Maréchal the previous night, I was quite certain he would find some way to murder me—if, indeed, he had not already attempted something of the sort on our way back through the periphery of the swamp. He had been afraid of witnesses, perhaps afraid of my maid's presence somewhere in those glades. Whatever the cause of my present safety, I knew that I must remain alert.

Meanwhile, I paid for the items we had purchased from the mercer and was about to leave with Darielle when two ladies bustled over to greet me. One introduced herself as a planter's wife and the other as the wife of the ship's chandler, who did a roaring business in Port Fleur. I lingered briefly to talk with them, wanting to be certain that Lieutenant Felipe was not hanging about outside.

As soon as I thought it safe, Darielle and I returned to the little park just off the Quai des Fleurs, and there we found the coachman, Shimbé, getting back onto his box, and the mare fretting impatiently. It was only then, as we clip-clopped up the cliff road around the bay to Government House, that I recalled I had been too concerned over the intrigue at the hut in Mourne Swamp to ask Agnes Mabberly what business she had had with my husband last night.

Of course, I knew the business. I had known it all along! And I was astonished at the violence of my own reaction to the picture of Agnes Mabberly in Ian's arms. In his bed. Where I belonged. It was true that Agnes Mabberly had known him first, but jealousy is seldom just in its resentments, and I kept wondering what it would be like to be loved by Ian Douglas.

By the time we had arrived at the semicircular drive in front of Government House, I was convinced that my long and somewhat harrowing trip to see Mrs.

Mabberly had disturbed no one unduly, except, of course, Lieutenant Felipe. But I had not reckoned with my husband.

Shimbé had just drawn up in front of the house when Ian Douglas charged out the door and across the portico with such enormous strides that he made me think of a West Indian hurricane. He wore a riding coat and top boots, and was calling to someone within the portico, whom I couldn't see. He wanted his horse saddled and his general conduct semed so dramatic I wanted to quote: "A horse! A horse! My kingdom . . ." and so on. "Set me down here," I ordered Shimbé, and leaped off almost before the steps were let down. My husband and I came abruptly face to face in the striped shadows of the portico. I had the advantage of being prepared for the encounter, but Ian was definitely startled, and the sight of me made him even angrier.

*"Where the devil have you been?"*

This husbandly greeting amused me so much that I leaned across the riding crop in his hand and kissed him lightly on the cheek. With all the false meekness I could muster, I said, "I have been shopping, Ian. You know how wives are when they find themselves turned out upon a shop full of trinkets and oddities."

His eyes blazed. I supposed he did not like to be made a figure of fun in the presence of his servants, and his answer matched his mood rather than mine.

"Madam, it would not be the first time a female of quality has been molested when she wandered off alone. It shall not happen to my wife. That I promise you."

I was struck by this very sensible argument and could not be angry with him. He passed me, still with the riding whip in hand, and I called after him lightly,

"Do not take out your temper upon the poor beast while your wife is available."

He paused, and for one heart-stopping moment I thought he would do precisely what I had suggested. Then his stiffened back relaxed a trifle. He looked over his shoulder at me, and when I applied my most innocent expression, he suddenly laughed. It was an abrupt, angry laugh, but a welcome sound.

I determined to make the first advance in mending the quarrel, and retraced my steps to offer him my hand.

"Are we quits, sir? Indeed, I am sorry I was so late. But you will see in the carriage how very many things there were to tempt a sedate London lady."

After a slight hesitation he took my gloved hand in his and appeared to study it as though my fingers might tell him something.

"Then you spent the entire time in the shops?"

"They are very intriguing shops."

He dropped my hand with such a rude, quick gesture that I wondered if I had somehow betrayed myself, or been betrayed by someone else. His smile was grim.

"Then it is lucky I am married to an heiress. We must have a talk about your fortune sometime. We—I may be in need of a considerable sum very soon. For the moment then, good day, my dear Madeline," and he was off to the stables for his ride. Every time he called me "my dear Madeline," I felt a prickle of sarcasm. I watched until he had mounted and galloped off on the South Coast Road which, I had been told, led all the way around the island.

His remark about my money was upsetting, but then, I had not supposed that he married me for my fatal charms. And I did wonder what purpose he had in mind for that "considerable sum" he would need. What sort of woman intrigued him? Did he have many mistresses? There was Agnes Mabberly, undoubtedly. How had he referred to her yesterday . . . an old friend? Something like that. Friend, indeed!

I walked on through the halls, with their strong rush of salt air and, more faintly, of flower scents mingled with the odor of sewage. I passed Tirsa on my way. The housekeeper was in the upper hall, only a step outside the chamber opposite my own suite, that chamber where, according to my maid Pepine, the French governor had kept his mistress.

"Should a late luncheon be set for you, madame? Luncheon was laid earlier in the expectation of Madame's return."

I felt all the guilt I had known in my childhood when I arrived late to a meal which Mama's cook had perhaps planned for hours. The difference was that Mama's soft reproach had aroused all my regrets, whereas Tirsa annoyed me because she was in the right, and yet did not reproach me directly. I began to remove my gloves as I walked briskly to the little salon of my suite.

"Tea and some fruit perhaps. No more."

I was afraid she would ask me about preparations for the evening, or whether I wished a certain gown and accessories laid out. I hadn't the remotest notion of what my husband wished me to do with the evening, and I certainly did not want Tirsa and the rest of the household to know that.

I started into my sitting room, became aware of the silence in the hall behind me, and stopped. The silence was strange, but I wasn't sure why I should find it so. Then I realized that I had been expecting to hear Tirsa's footsteps as she left the room across the hall.

She had not walked away, then, but only stepped back into the room. I turned to watch her and could not miss the proprietary look she gave to that chamber. But there was something else in that look, some emotion kept forcibly concealed. Yet the realization of its presence gripped me, tightening my throat: that emotion was longing; she was suffering a feeling of loss.

And then I knew that Tirsa, this quiet serving woman with her hostile superiority, had been the mistress of Government House when it was under French rule. I went into my own rooms, shaken by that knowledge, and made the more uneasy over my own usurpation of her place in this house.

Pepine came to me shortly after with Indian tea, appetizing little cakes freshly baked, and an assortment of fruit which would have made it unnecessary to eat again for days. And as she had this morning, Pepine brought me the news.

"Madame's relation, Captain Adare, has returned from his search of the island. He asks if you will see him very soon."

I was suddenly aware that I had neglected him. "Of course. I haven't seen George since the ball. Please ask if he will join me."

He must have been waiting immediately outside the door, for Pepine had scarcely left me when he came loping in. He saluted me in his casual way, but his manner was not as easy as usual. He seemed nervous, and I wondered if the search and its failure had affected him so much.

"Well, old girl, it's been a busy twenty-four hours, eh?"

"Sit down and help me devour this feast. Tell me about your search, George. Have you discovered the truth about that accident on the *Maud Vester?*"

"No, damn it! And old Ian's going to want to know why. Lieutenant Felipe went off God knows where last night, and left the rest of us to wallow in those damned mud flats this side of Boiling Lake. Found a deal of hostility. They're all for this rebel fellow, you know. But we didn't locate that sailor. I wonder what he was really up to. Can't imagine what he had against me, to make the rogue behave in such a fashion. I've been thinking and thinking, and I just can't figure what I could have done. Unless, of course—" He looked at me hopefully, "the entire affair really was an accident. Damn! Why not, Madeline? A simple, clumsy accident!"

"It seems likely," I said, hoping he would proceed on this route, since it might eventually cause them all to give up the search. Even so, George was still nervous. His feet kept tapping the table leg until I wanted to give him a sharp setdown. But I managed, with difficulty, to smile and suggest he take the matter more calmly.

"All very well, m'dear, but your life hasn't been threatened."

"Not necessarily." I would have despised myself if I had not the courage to remind him. "The man may have tried to kill me, not you, George." Having gone this slight way in honesty, I felt I might throw a veil across the actual reasons for an attack on me. "After all, as Governor Douglas's betrothed, I might have been a good target for one of Le Maréchal's men."

"No. 'Fraid you don't understand, old girl. Not that business yesterday. Quite another matter. Nothing but superstition, of course. Silly, if you ask me. But there it is." He unintentionally dropped a smooth brown banana skin on my fingers, and I shivered. Something was coming, something else unpleasant. His attitude was very uncharacteristic. George had not enough imagination to be frightened, yet there he was, his fly-away red hair almost standing up on his skull. He put his hand into his breeches pocket stealthily, without looking down.

"George, what under heaven ails you? What are you hiding?"

Forgetting myself, I reached across the table, reliving the days when we were children together and I had probably been overbearing and horrid to my easygoing cousin.

Sheepishly, he withdrew his hand. In it was a curious toy made of bright cloth and wood. A doll, of all things.

"What a charming little doll! Wherever did you get it?"

"Found it in my napkin at luncheon. Madeline, did you ever hear of something called voodoo?"

My hand retreated slowly.

"A custom the slaves follow, isn't it? A religion for those who aren't Christian, I suppose. Is that doll one of the things they worship?" I studied it with rising interest. "I should imagine it might be like the Christ Child to them."

The late-afternoon brightness was fading in a burning sunset. For a few moments every object in the room was illuminated in a crystal-clear light before the evening shadows blurred them. George frowned, and flicked the doll with a thumb and forefinger.

"No, I think the thing would be black, if it represented something to them. Besides, this doesn't appear to be a baby. No face to it—no features, that is. Nothing worth mentioning, but it's a grownup figure."

It was carved from some heavy, fine-grained wood, very dark. Oddly enough, the face, or what appeared to be the face, was painted a pale, milky white. The doll stood about the height of my hand, the carving unskilled. The arms and legs were mere splinters worked into holes in the trunk. Then I began to examine the costume, a circular bit of muslin representing a skirt.

George cleared his throat. "Voodoo isn't exactly a religion, though it's part of the *houngans'*—the voodoo priests'—ceremony. But it's not the way we see religion. A doll like this is a sign of death. You see the hair bodkin that somebody's stuck into the throat, or what passes for the throat—that little stick there. That is a curse. The *houngans* who run all this sort of thing have put a solemn curse upon objects brought to them for the purpose. And the funny thing is, almost invariably the damned curse is fulfilled by the victim himself. What the doll says is that the person it's meant for is dying. But what reason have the locals for killing me, except as a member of the new government? Unless it's that sailor who caused the trouble yesterday. Yet there it was, in my napkin when I unfolded it."

"But it is obviously a female. How could it represent you?" I broke off, and we looked steadily at each other. Then I picked up the doll, weighed it in my palm. Several details began to fit into a pattern. "George, was the table set especially for you?"

"Already set. I happened in, had to report to old Ian—thank God I missed him. Gives me a little time to compose suitable reasons for our failure. At all events, there was the table set, and me half-starved. The good Tirsa agreed there'd be no objection to my dining here, since I am, in a manner of speaking, the governor's cousin now."

"Good God!" I dropped the doll. It seemed to burn my fingertips.

"Madeline, old girl, what ails you? Stop staring at that damned toy."

The room was shot with queer lights and shadows, the terrible brilliance of the dying sun giving way to the creeping night that would follow. I thought of these things because I did not want to concentrate upon the truth.

The lunch George had eaten was my lunch. The napkin was set for me. And so was the death doll.

# *10*

"It is the housekeeper, I'm afraid," I said after that little silence between us.

"Tirsa? Rubbish! She has no reason to put her witch doctors onto you."

"She was the mistress of this house before the English came."

He glanced around uneasily as if half expecting to find the quiet, capable woman standing at his back.

"Not Tirsa. It's true that she was the French governor's mistress, but why would she have let me eat at that place setting? If Tirsa had put the idiotic doll there for you, she would have removed it before I ate, or at least seen that I didn't sit at that particular place."

"Perhaps she didn't care," I ventured. "Perhaps it was simply a way to even the score with the foreigners, the English."

"Then why not threaten old Ian? He's their real enemy. You and I are only a small part of it."

There was much merit in his argument. But if not Tirsa, then who had done this thing? If Lieutenant Felipe were somewhere about Government House, I might have suspected him of trying to frighten me into silence by this absurd threat. The difficulty was, I could not believe his methods would be so primitive.

Some other enemy, then.

George sighed. He started to replace the doll in his breeches pocket, caught my glance, and grinned sheepishly.

"Was it for me? Or for you, old girl? Either way, is it worth going into all this gloom?"

I touched his hand in the old easy way of our childhood, welcoming his common sense.

"Thank you, George. Take that idiotic doll and throw it in the bay. Here! We will do it now. I'll open the window."

I pushed the window outward, and George came over behind me to look at the view exposed there in all its tropic glory. The water far below glistened with myriad broken lights and shadows. As on the previous day, the bay appeared to be burning, the flames of sunset licking at the heavy cliff base, the foundations of Government House. I could almost feel the heat of the flames as the tide swept in upon a ledge below the foundations.

George took the doll and held it out over the water, then looked at me. "What say?"

"Out!"

We watched the downward course of the witch doll, seeing a vagrant sea wind briefly carry the fluttering thing outward, but in the end it plummeted into those burning waters, and I was relieved when I could no longer make out the hateful object.

George laughed. "That's done for. No more complaints on that score."

Somewhat to my surprise, he returned to the little table and began to eat another of the fruits laid before my plate with the small, gleaming knife beside it.

"Good heavens!" I remarked lightly. "You ate my

luncheon belowstairs, and now you are hungry for my tea abovestairs."

He peeled the ripe green globe of the fruit, cut slices, and popped them into his mouth.

"Tell you the truth, Madeline, after I found that cursed doll, I lost my appetite."

I very nearly laughed, but realized in time that I too was affected, in spite of common sense, and I could not make him a figure of fun over the fears I shared. I watched him finish, for I had lost my own appetite, then accompanied him to the sitting-room door when he left.

"Shall we see you at dinner, George?"

"See me?" He gave a quick "ha!" of laughter. "Shall you see that infernal husband of yours? That is more to the point. Is he off searching for Le Maréchal, or merely for that clumsy-handed sailor?"

"I wish I knew. And you are quite right. I've no notion whether he will join me at dinner or not. I don't think he is out on official business, though. He wasn't in uniform. Perhaps he went riding for the exercise." *And to avoid me,* I thought ruefully, but did not say so.

He shrugged. "Actually no concern of mine. Got to be getting over to headquarters. Late already. Ta-ta."

His absurd little remarks, gestures, and salutes always affected me in one way or another. When I wanted to be serious and my cousin did not, I was annoyed. But at times like this, when I felt that dangers were closing in upon me from all sides, I was pleased that he could cheer me up.

The suite was gray with twilight now, and all the unfamiliar furnishings took on eerie new shapes around me. I went to the nearest window, leaned upon the sill, and studied the waters of the bay. The air was busy with large birds which I took to be vultures diving for dead or discarded fish. A pleasant breeze cooled my skin, and after a few minutes I was in control of my emotions once more.

At least I thought I was, until I heard the door from the corridor to the sitting room opened without a knock or warning of any kind. I swung around, aware of my quickened heartbeat.

"Who is there?"

Pepine's low voice replied. I was not greatly reassured.

"I am here to light the candles, madame." She came into the bedchamber, and I stood with my back to the window as I watched her. Already there was a pleasant glow from the burning branch of candles on the commode, when Pepine suddenly shook me badly by uttering an ear-splitting scream. She pointed to me.

"What is it? For God's sake, what ails you?" My voice sharp and highpitched, revealed how superficial had been the calmness of moments ago.

"The window, Madame!"

I swung around. One of the great birds had dived so close to the open window that it might have flown in but for the brightness of the light from the candles.

I tried a feeble laugh. "One of those horrid scavengers, I suppose. I don't think vultures attack people . . do they?"

Pepine moistened her lips. She was obviously shaken.

"N-no. Only if the body is dead. But that was a bat. They fly at night here. Over the jungles. They live on the blood of cattle and sheep that graze on the south coast." She repeated nervously, "The—the blood."

"But not human blood."

"As to that—" Her delicately shaped eyebrows lifted in that piquant face which now had a pinched look. "Who is to say, madame? If they find one form of blood to their taste—"

"Pepine! Really!"

She looked somewhat abashed, and finished her chore. As she was leaving, she appeared to remember a message somewhat belatedly.

"Monsieur the Governor asks me to inform you that dinner will be served at seven and you are expected to appear."

How peculiar this marriage was, from its beginnings at the Mairie yesterday to the haughty pronouncement tonight!

"You may convey to Monsieur the Governor the information that Madame the Governor's wife conceives it her duty to appear at dinner with His Excellency, and will duly appear upon the hour named."

Pepine opened her mouth, began with a glazed look, "Madame the Governor's Wife conceives it her duty . . ." and lost the thread.

"I have no doubt that you will convey the essence of my words," I said, and closed the door after her.

I immediately set about examining my wardrobe for a gown suitable for the evening's dinner. It would be an important occasion for me, since my husband's indifference, as well as his undeniable attractions, made me determined to arouse his interest in me as a woman.

I was not satisfied that any of my gowns suited my mood, and ended by choosing last year's white gown with a silver gauze shawl and silver ornaments in my hair and earlobes. By the time Darielle and another young girl arrived to assist me I was certain that I had made a bad choice, but I was too proud to admit to myself—or reveal to them—that my new husband's opinion mattered so much to me.

By the time the girls considered me ready, I had three or four minutes in which to make my way down to the dining salon in the south half of the ground floor public rooms. With the friendly and helpful Darielle watching from the open hall above, I descended the stairs, hoping my husband might have that special look in his eyes that I had noted and been moved by on the previous night. But this magic was unlikely to happen a second time and at the foot of the stairs I was still quite alone.

I lifted my chin and with a long breath and short steps, walked toward the closed doors of the dining salon. He was making this very difficult. Those closed double doors must have been his idea, for they usually stood open. I glanced at the exquisite ormolu clock with its overlay of bronze that made it send off rich sparks before the great mirror which was its frame. One minute before seven. I waited.

Somewhere on this floor another clock chimed the hour exactly as I put my hands upon the latches of both salon doors. I heard a servant rushing along behind me to oblige, but I had already thrown open the doors as the clock stopped chiming.

Ian Douglas had been standing across the room, looking out the long window at the bay beyond when the doors burst open. I was delighted that I had startled him. When he turned around to face me he scowled, an expression I was rapidly coming to believe had been fixed upon his face at birth. I sank in a curtsey, all politeness, to tease him by my sweet compliance with his orders.

"Good evening, sir."

Recovering his poise, he came forward, took my hand, and escorted me to the place near his own chair at the head of—the absurdly long table covered by beautiful napery, silver and glassware. In those seconds I sneaked a look at him, and was eminently satisfied with what I saw. He was not in uniform but wore a frock coat and breeches, silk hose, and pumps, with a muscular arrogance that shook me a little. My life had been singularly empty of such intensely masculine appeal. The immaculate white of his cravat beneath that haughty chin only added to the impression of a man's man who would be doubly attractive to women.

Seating me, he remarked, "You are a rare woman, indeed!"

Ah! Better. Much better. I smiled with all the warmth I had been storing for just such an instant. "Thank you—er—Ian. But in what way am I rare?"

"You were prompt to the second. It has been my experience that promptness is all too rare in females."

Flat. A distinct setdown. My smile wavered, but I was determined to try again. While we were being served by still another servant, whom I did not remember seeing before, I ventured, "Did you have a pleasant ride today?"

He looked at me and laughed. "Very pleasant, since it was not necessary to go off at a cavalry charge to rescue my lost wife. I kept picturing you at the receiving end of my riding crop."

We laughed together, a heavenly moment all too unusual in our relationship thus far.

Our amusement faded. I caught him studying my face, my throat, perhaps my earrings, and then my bosom. It was my own fault—my gown was shockingly low-cut. I tried hard not to color, a habit I thought I had broken long ago. I moistened my lips and tried to concentrate on my dinner plate and the elaborate crystal service.

My husband remarked suddenly, "I wonder if I haven't gotten a better bargain than I deserve."

I took up my glass. "You can hardly be certain of that while we are at this distance, sir."

He laughed. "That shall be mended."

For an instant it looked as if we might begin this new relationship then and there, but another of the ubiquitous servants was upon us with a new course, and we had to turn our attention to the matter at hand.

We spoke only of unimportant things, never touching on our actual concerns, but I remember thinking that this was how the ideal marriage was conducted and enjoyed. Mama and Father had been very like this, and they were certainly happy. How wonderful and how unexpected if Ian Douglas and I could enjoy something of that closeness ourselves.

But our ideal marriage—so different from any we might have had in the elegant promiscuity of London society under its leader, the Prince of Wales—was not destined to begin that night. We had not yet come to my husband's after-dinner Madeira and cigars when the butler, stately and unbending, came in to whisper something to him in confidence.

He arose at once, shoving back his chair with a grating noise. I winced at the irritating scrape of the chair, but was more concerned over the news which had sent Ian into such activity. I hoped he would give me some hint before leaving me, but whether it was his habit to keep cautiously silent, or he merely thought me an addlepated gossip, he said nothing beyond making his excuses. He took my hand and held it as he spoke.

"I daresay you will be relieved by my not thrusting

my presence upon you this evening, my dear Madeline. I was churlish about my dinner summons and you have behaved beautifully. Which no longer surprises me." He caressed my fingers lightly. "I only ask that you behave discreetly. I trust to your judgment in such matters."

What the devil was he talking about?

"Naturally, I shall be discreet," I said. "I have always been discreet. Of necessity." I hadn't supposed he would understand those final cryptic words, but his reaction was alarmingly stiff, and those dark, dangerous-looking eyes stared at me for an instant.

"Yes, I rather imagine a lady of your character must be discreet. *Of necessity.*" There was no mistaking the twist of dislike, almost hatred, in that remark. He added, heavily sarcastic, "And, discreet as you are, my beautiful and wholly undeserved wife, you would come as easily to me as to another if I summoned you."

Puzzled at his violent change of mood, I wondered if he could be drunk without my having guessed. I laughed my scorn as I reminded him, "I already have, have I not?"

He dropped my hand and walked out of the room. I stood up, thinking to make one more effort at peace before he left, but was shocked to see Lieutenant Felipe waiting outside the open double doors of the dining room. I remained in the doorway, and when the lieutenant glanced back at me with his hooded eyes and small, respectful smile, I managed to say brightly, "Good evening, Lieutenant. Please take good care of my husband. We all depend upon you to protect him from harm, especially from dangerous traps."

Ian Douglas would have been furious if he had heard this, but I was trying to warn Lieutenant Felipe that if anything happened to his governor, he would be held accountable. I believe he took my meaning. His moist smile broadened and he bowed, but his eyes did not reflect those smiling lips.

I lingered in the long, formal hall, staring at the lovely ormolu clock, the long mirror, the commodes with their candle branches and bowls of flowers, but I thought of these objects as mere adjuncts to the life of any woman who happened to be the governor's wife. I had neglected the matter of my own house in London, which was now my husband's property. The furnishings were fully as rich and elaborate as these; something must be done about selling the house.

But I made a curious discovery as I examined these beautiful objects: I could be quite happy with Ian Douglas in a soldier's barracks life. If, of course, I could disabuse him of his absurd notions about me and turn him into a reasonably civil man, the kind he had been at dinner tonight.

Tirsa's straight-backed form appeared on the portico, and I walked through the reception hall to join her. My presence seemed completely unexpected, but she was her usual polite self. She looked very tired and even worried, I thought. I tried to make my tone relaxed and easy, a talk between two women, not a business discussion between mistress and servant. Or worse—mistress and slave.

When my mundane remarks about the weather brought a noncommittal response, I turned to the subject of the island and its products, then asked if she felt that the governor was putting forth his best efforts for St. Sebastien.

"I am not in a position to judge, madame," she said quietly. "My business is with his personal comforts." She paused just long enough for me to be aware of her hesitation, then added, "As well as those of his family."

"Yes. I understand. And the governor considers you—"

But she was gone. The painful thing was that I sympathized with Tirsa and yet was incapable of saying the right thing. Perhaps there was no right thing that one could say to the former mistress of the house.

It was too hot to go back inside the house. I stood there a few minutes longer to avoid humiliation, for I saw Tirsa at the window of one of the small receiving salons as she reached out to close the shutters. Then I strolled to the end of the portico, stepped away from the house, and moved past the outside kitchen where slaves were cleaning up after our abortive dinner. Beyond the kitchen the ground was more open, and cool air drifted across from the outer bay. I was grateful for this refreshing air, as my throat felt parched and hot.

Until I aroused Luc Monceau's enmity, I had never minded being alone. Yet in this hot, flower-scented tropic night, I found myself nervously looking around, peering into shadows, jumping when a leaf rustled.

On a leveled area at the top of the cliff I found a great pit with coals still smouldering. But no one seemed to be around, and only a few steps beyond the edge of this clearing was the vanguard of the jungle, huge vegetation which looked too thick to be a mere forest of tropical trees. These green monsters with their massive leaves and heavily rooted trunks were more like plants grown to unnatural size. I did not stray too close to them in these night shadows. Indeed, so thickly were they interwoven that even a full moon could have sent through scarcely a sliver of light.

The road around the southeastern half of the island lay before me in the starlight, seeming brighter by contrast with the black of the jungle. Figures moved along that road, away from Government House, having completed their day's work. The sight surprised me a little; I had supposed the governor's servants lived at the house, but perhaps they preferred to live elsewhere.

I must have been more anxious about my relationship with my husband than I had supposed, for my nerves were tight. Tight enough so that there was almost a pain in my breast—no, my throat. The pain of anxiety, of course. I took long, labored breaths, hating to return to the house with its layers of heavily scented heat. More servants left the house—the butler and a woman I did not recognize. I stayed in the shadows, but in my gaudy white and silver gown I could scarcely expect to remain unseen. Yet when these two passed, they looked straight into the darkness, and stared at me with blank faces. But perhaps it was my imagination or the starlight, which made their eyes glitter in their dark faces. They shone with hostility, I thought. Then I remembered their outlaw hero, and understood.

Little things—the possible antagonism of strangers, a nagging dislike of the coming hours to be spent alone in a household in which I was an alien—were undoubtedly the cause of that tightening in my throat, that sense of choking. I felt an actual pain stabbing at the chords that stiffened in my neck—I badly needed a drink of water, although I had already been warned about the island's water supply. It was meager and seemed to bring disease. But there were moments when nothing was so satisfactory as water.

I started back to the light and shadow of the portico, and had nearly reached the open front doors, when I heard the hoofbeats of a horse approaching along the South Coast Road.

Ian Douglas? Astonished at my own pleasure and relief, I swung around and started back out to the road, only to see one of my husband's black lieutenants thundering up to the portico on a sweating mount. Before I reached him, the lieutenant called to me in French.

"Madame! Monsieur the Governor has been shot. A sniper in ambush. We need cloth, wrappings . . . a powder to close the wound. . . ."

Having heard the arrival, Shimbé came out of his cabin in bedgown and bare feet, obligingly taking the reins from the breathless rider. The lieutenant dismounted while I quickly went into the house, calling to Tirsa. The young lieutenant was close behind me. As we hurried, I asked, "How bad is the wound? Where is its location?"

"The shoulder, but very near to the breastbone, madame. It is serious but not fatal, I believe. That is for the surgeon to say."

"You have sent for a surgeon, then?"

"In a village on the south coast, yes. Doubtless a follower of Le Maréchal, but satisfactory, we are told."

I led him along the lower floor to the housekeeper's quarters, questioning him all the while.

"Where did it happen? One of Le Maréchal's men, I don't doubt."

"Possibly a French rebel, madame. But it occurred on the mule path across the island."

The door of the housekeeper's quarters opened abruptly. Tirsa stood before us. There was no need of our explaining again. She held an armful of neatly ironed linen.

"A pinafore used by one of the girls." She began to tear it into strips. In the crook of her arm was a glass jar. "Basilicum powder," she explained. "Effective upon wounds when the injury has been cleansed."

I thanked her and held out my hands, but she gave the cloth and the jar to the young soldier.

"I will return with you, Lieutenant Aaba. I know the countryside and I have experience of such matters."

"No! Please! I want to help my husband. You must understand, Tirsa. And *I* have had experience. My father was once stabbed by a footpad. . . . Lieutenant Aaba, please come."

I half-expected Tirsa's anger, her resentment. It was much more disturbing when she reached out one of those competent hands.

"Madame, it is better if I go. The mule trail crosses the north shore of Boiling Lake. It is no place for a white lady. Let me go in your stead."

I looked at her for an instant. "I must."

Again there was that unexpected compassion in her eyes. "I understand, madame."

She made no further effort to stop us, but as we left the house after I changed into the heavy, hooded cloak I had worn through the rough weather at sea, I was troubled not only by my husband's danger, but by the curious pity in the housekeeper's eyes.

# 11

"Monsieur's carriage is best to take," the lieutenant suggested. "Then he may be brought back in more comfort. Do you not agree, madame?"

"If the mule track you mention is wide enough."

"You may depend upon me, madame."

I assumed his answer meant yes, and agreed it would be better for my husband, but my opinion apparently mattered very little: Shimbé, having lighted the carriage lamps, was already harnessing the horses. We sprang up into the carriage, Lieutenant Aaba assisting me, and then the lieutenant elbowed Shimbé aside and took his place on the box.

Already the town of Port Fleur was dark, with only a cluster of small lights here and there blinking in the night breeze. I wondered briefly if Agnes Mabberly knew of my husband's injury. Had anyone notified this old "friend" of Ian's, this woman whom he visited on the very night of his marriage to me?

I peered into the unknown dark, wondering. Even now, I felt myself under constant observation from unseen creatures, human or otherwise, who might be hiding in that darkness.

"Do you know my husband well?" I asked, directing my question to Lieutenant Aaba's back as we moved rapidly onto a wider, obviously much-used road, which led southward. In a matter of minutes we were moving between the great palms and twisted jungle vegetation that smelled of rain. Although the heat around Government House was humid, there was no indication of approaching rain, yet here, so short a distance away, the palm fronds and giant elephant leaves dripped on my head, and the air was thick with moisture.

I had to repeat my question before the lieutenant understood me. He was peering anxiously into the tropic night that enclosed us.

"I know Monsieur the Governor only from the conquest of St. Sebastien, madame. I was a loyal soldier in the service of the French Republic. Now I am His Excellency's man."

I understood, and liked him no less for his frankness. I started to ask about the circumstances of my husband's injury when a hideous creature appeared to explode out of the jungle darkness—a nightmarelike bird that nearly blinded one of the horses as it swooped past. It must have been a bat. I closed my eyes and cried out before I could stop myself. I knew immediately that my cry had been stupid and dangerous; it might warn Le Maréchal's sympathizers that someone was approaching. And what if they discovered it was their enemy's wife, almost unattended at this late hour? Still, they could scarcely miss me in the carriage on the public road. I raised my head and looked around. I fancied I could see eyes in all the underbrush lining the road. Eyes gleaming at me. I stiffened and tried to turn my thoughts quickly to a matter of much more vital importance: my husband's life.

We passed only one traveler moving in our direction, a native woman with an ancient nag, that still had not its owner's years. By the time the moon rose, the road had branched into two trails scarcely wide enough to make room for the four wagon wheels. We turned eastward. The jungle vegetation rapidly entangled us. Great wet tentacles first wound about Lieutenant Aaba's lean body, and he struggled to release himself with one hand while the other controlled the reins. Then I began to claw my way out of that slimy embrace. At last it became clear that the horses found the going almost impossible.

"We will have to walk," I called to him as we bounced along, the wheels spinning ever deeper into mud and rotted plant and animal life. I would not think of what walking in this foul swamp might entail. "The horses can't go much further. The road is turning to swamp."

"It is so," he said, and leaped down. His boots sank into a morass, and neither the carriage lights nor the faint moon's rays gave us much indication of what was solid ground and what was swamp. The lieutenant called out in angry terror, and I seized his groping hands, trying to prevent him from slipping into the faintly rustling, faintly sighing depths behind him.

"You should never have brought the carriage and horses through here," I cried, too late to do any good. But I could not imagine why he had done so. The veriest stranger like myself would know at once that it was impossible to move the horses much further in this direction.

Clutching my hands, he finally managed to recover his balance. But the carriage rocked under our swaying weight, and the lieutenant made his way carefully to the horses' heads, calming the panicked beasts.

"Can we leave them here and go on?" I called as I

studied the trail. It was swallowed up in foliage only a minute's walk ahead of us. We should not, in any case, be able to judge further than a few steps at a time. ·

The lieutenant suddenly flung his arms over his head, frightening off another of the repulsive night-flying creatures. I could have sworn I saw the bat's little red eyes as it flew over my head, and its flapping wings were audible somewhere among the trees and foliage that closed us in. I shuddered at the idea that this suggested.

"We cannot leave the horses here. Those accursed bats will drain them," I said.

I was exceedingly impatient with the lieutenant for his stupidity over the carriage and horses. It was he, and not I, who should have thought about the danger to the horses out here in the swamp.

*But then, perhaps he had.*

I hadn't spent my life serving the political interests of a spying organization without being myself a woman of suspicious nature. I had been a fool to follow the unknown Lieutenant Aaba. I would be a greater fool to continue in my first mistake. But if possible, I would not let him know that I was suspicious. And there was always the possibility that my husband actually was injured and lying somewhere in this ghastly swamp, waiting for help from me and from the surgeon they might or might not have located in the village on the south coast.

I obeyed my instincts rather than my sympathies and my anxiety over Ian Douglas's welfare. My instincts had never failed me so far as I knew. This time, of course, might be the exception.

I glanced quickly to see if there were pistols in the pocket beside the coachman's box, as there would be in an English carriage. Nothing glistened in the moonlight. The lieutenant was undoubtedly armed, but his hands were full at present as he soothed the horses.

I watched Lieutenant Aaba and decided that he was waiting too, borrowing time, doubtless because we had reached this spot too soon. He listened. As I watched him, he slowed his movements and cocked his head a little. I needed no more to be certain. I moved very slightly, enough to get a better view of the coachman's box, and wished I might examine more closely that pocket where the coachman's pistol should have been located. Unless the lieutenant had removed it, there should also be a knife in that pocket, to extricate the carriage or horses from their harness in case of accident.

"Are the wheels imbedded in mud?" I called to the lieutenant, using the opportunity to stand and reach into the box pocket while he examined the front wheels. I knew a moment of sickening terror when my hand found nothing, but I did not want him to suspect.

"I had best join you and we will walk to the Boiling Lake," I told him, far more calmly than I felt. "We must get on." Suiting the action to the words, I managed to climb over the side opposite that place in the quivering mud where Lieutenant Aaba appeared to be at work. I kept talking, giving silly advice, complaining about the damage to my white skirts, now hopelessly mired, and my black kid slippers. It was fortunate I had changed these, but this too came of a lifetime's training. I had often been called upon at odd hours to go somewhere with Mama or Father, and good sturdy slippers were a necessity.

As I watched him from the darkness of the swamp's edge, giant ferns groped around my hair and the back of my neck. I drew the hood over my head again and moved stealthily away. Lieutenant Aaba was expecting someone to approach from the east, further along the swamp trail. His listening attitude, his attention fixed upon that black morass, convinced me.

I made another inane remark to prolong his belief in my gullibility, then moved silently past the carriage. By the time I had covered myself completely, shrouded in the old storm cloak, and moved within the confines of the swamp, he could no longer see me at all. He had not yet called to me in panic, so I wasn't missed. I knew the general direction back to the South Coast Road, and by making my way along the outer edge of the jungle vegetation beside the swamp trail, I felt I could reach some kind of civilization in a short time. Meanwhile, I was grateful for the eerie gulping, gasping noises of the swamp, for they covered the sound of my own feet pulling with difficulty through the pools of twigs and rotten foliage.

I had made my way for some time when I heard Lieutenant Aaba call out my name from surprisingly far away. I remained still, although the plant world around me was more restless than ever. Just as I had satisfied myself that my position was not suspected, something passed gently over both my insteps. A ray or two of the rising moon flashed upon the graceful, shimmering length of a snake. To my horrified gaze, its size was enormous, and I dared not move. How many of its fellows lurked among the thick reeds in which I stood? I had never so passionately wanted to shriek. But the creature had proved to be harmless to me, thus far.

With a long breath I stepped out into the trail, which was now fairly illuminated by the moon overhead. I began to run. I must have been close to the South Coast Road when the most inexplicable thing of that terrible night occurred. I ran into an invisible barrier that felt as thin as a spider's web but sent me sprawling to the ground; it was a cord stretched across the trail from one tree limb to another.

Breathless and aching, I tried to pick myself up from the wagon ruts of the trail, but before I could rise, at least a half dozen hands seized me.

A voice called in French, "Gently! Or she will be no use to us!" Alarmed as I was, my instincts told me that whoever these men might be, they did not intend to murder me at once. My second fear, that they might assault me, was slightly allayed by the leader's instructions. I suspected that a political maneuver was in their minds, but before I could identify any of them— assuming that was possible—I was roughly stood on my feet while cold, muscular hands bound a piece of home-spun over my eyes.

"Did you expect me to escape from the lieutenant? Were you waiting for me?" I asked in English, in a voice that quavered and sounded surprisingly gruff to my own ears. I hoped that something might be gained if they did not know I spoke fluently in my mother's tongue.

"She's a head on her shoulders and a heart for a rough game," someone said in French. Then he explained to me in broken English, "Madame was not expected. The cord was to catch anyone who followed Madame and Lieutenant Aaba."

"Be quiet!" a deeper voice ordered. "You talk too much! If she guesses one of you, she cannot be sent back alive." The ease and quiet certainty with which this was spoken set me shivering.

I was sure now that the plan was to abduct me for some political gain to Le Maréchal's cause. If I wanted to remain alive through this ordeal, I must watch my every movement and not attempt anything absurd.

They shoved me along between two of the men, back over the path I had crossed with such an effort. They had not troubled to conceal their direction: they must suppose I would never dare to make a sudden break for freedom. Indeed, they were quite correct! As soon as I became used to the bandage across my eyes, I found that some faint light came through the homespun. I could also see my feet and a bit of the ground when the foliage did not shut out all the moonlight.

I was relieved that they had not bound my arms, nor used more force than was necessary to keep me marching along the trail between them. They walked in a long, loping stride, the easy, athletic walk of the black natives of St. Sebastien. But although I walked very rapidly for a female, tonight I was handicapped by the narrow skirts I wore. I stumbled several times over my skirts until the hem ripped about my ankles. Shocking as the revelation of my ankles might be to the ladies of London, I was better able to keep pace with my captors.

By the time we reached what I assumed to be Lieutenant Aaba, I no longer listened to all their chattering among themselves. I was not nearly so frightened. I had decided that I would be safe at least until my return to Government House was negotiated. It was all a political affair, and my life would depend upon some concession made by my husband. Surely, no matter how much Ian Douglas disliked me, he would think my life worth saving! While I was debating this in my stumbling, blindfolded state, I heard another voice behind me—a French-speaking voice I had not noticed before, soft, almost whispering, but audible to me in its direct and terrible meaning.

"Useless to speak of returning the woman. Luc Monceau's agent said Monceau would offer five hundred guineas. It is too much to refuse. And we need the goodwill of the French. Think what can be done for the liberation with five hundred guineas, and the Frenchman's cooperation. Already he has allowed this sailor to deliver money for weapons. And five hundred guineas more—we can even buy from the Yankees."

One of my captors murmured with a horrible kind of reasonableness, "Still, it is not so easy. Murder, yes. A simple thing. But the body of a white female—the governor's wife? It must never be found. The whole Caribbean would be in arms."

"Why would it be found?"

While I felt my flesh crawl with such fear as I had never known, I heard the reply, reluctant and given with a sigh by someone else. "The leader makes the decision, as always."

My life then depended upon a whim. But there must be some way, something. I might outbid them. Outbid Luc Monceau's agent on St. Sebastien, whoever he or she might be. One of those agents was the sailor, Peter Phipps. But was there another? Phipps's delirious words had certainly suggested as much. I must be incurably optimistic, but I could not believe I was actually being discussed as a clumsy packet of goods whose disposal would cause more trouble than my murder.

Bribery, I thought . . . but bribery conducted in such a manner as to ensure my rescue before full payment was made. How to handle that? In either case I must outbid Monceau's agent. Perhaps now, in this ghastly predicament, I would know at last who was my real antagonist on St. Sebastien. Much good the knowledge would do me if I died before being released. And to die such a death . . . in these stinking, muddy swamps!

Again speaking in English, I ventured to whoever might be paying attention, "It is possible I can help your leader more than you can."

This jarred the captor who held my left arm just above the elbow in a pinching grip.

"How is this, ma'am?"

"Because the former government, the French Republic, will help you. And I can contact them." Then I could not go on. In all my hurry to escape Luc Monceau's long hand, I had never really thought what it was like to be a traitor. I had betrayed Monceau to preserve my life and because I hated him for causing other agents to be murdered. Could I now betray my husband's government and mine, by calling upon the previous government of St. Sebastien and perhaps permitting their agents to undo all that Ian was attempting to build up?

"You say others will help Le Maréchal, ma'am? You are acquainted with these French?"

The struggle within me did not last long because I forced myself to deny the cowardly call to my old loyalties.

"No. I merely suggested what you must know. But my goodwill should be worth something. I believe in Le Maréchal. I could be of great assistance to him in Government House."

But they were not naive. They sputtered contemptuous laughter as someone repeated my words in French. By this time we were passing in single file around the Government House carriage. The horses appeared to be gone, probably unharnessed and removed by Lieutenant Aaba. From an equine whiffer of protest by one of the animals ahead of us on the trail, I suspected they too were being delivered to Le Maréchal somewhere in the center of the island: one governor's wife plus two carriage horses. Three fairly substantial gifts for the rebel leader.

I wondered idly what had become of the wrappings and Basilicum powder I had left in the carriage. I wondered too if, by the time the sun rose over this hopeless morass of swamp and jungle, I would already have been dead for several hours. My situation still seemed unreal. Death from a plunging, runaway team in London, or a hired footpad, or even a strangler who had broken into my London house. But not here in this fetid world of rotting beauty . . . Such a fate was worse than any I had feared at the hands of Luc Monceau's agents. But then, the murderers among my captors were Luc Monceau's agents. I had no doubt that the one who had offered them five hundred guineas came direct from Monceau.

And to die without ever having been understood by my husband! That seemed the worst of my fears now. Why had I not told him straight out that he was wrong in his apparent suspicions of me, of my visits to lovers, or whatever he thought I was doing? It had amused me to tantalize him, but I felt that there was something between us, some deep sensation of desire that might, in time, become love. Was it all too late now?

We came to a sudden halt. I thought we had arrived at the rebel leader's encampment, but I was shoved to one side, and warm, sweating hands bound my wrists behind me. I was grateful that the binding cord at least had not numbed my hands. I remembered a trick Father said was used years before in Ireland when a man bound hand and foot was able to release himself, having expanded and contracted his muscles at exactly the right moments. I was not so skilled, but I had managed a slight effort to expand the muscles of my wrists. And I was ever hopeful. The alternatives did not bear thinking of.

The journey obviously grew more dangerous here. I made out small strips of light across the ground, which only punctuated the great dark that engulfed the jungle. One sliver of light revealed what appeared to be a vast pit on my right. We made our way along the crumbling, muddy border for several minutes, carefully putting one foot before the other. The cord that bound my wrists was held by someone behind me. Probably if I slipped and fell toward that ominous pit far below, the captor behind me would drag me back to safety, but by that time I might be badly injured.

The tightness that had troubled my throat returned. Certainly a sign of the agitation I had tried to hide. Different and more powerful odors reached me now. Mud, of course, and dead plant and animal life, but there was more than mud in that great churning pit on our right, there was something that smelled like burning oil. Lava might smell like this, I thought, although I had no way of knowing. I was once almost overpowered by the smoke from a London fire in which stones, mortar, and wood all seemed to melt in the awful heat. So it was in this place. Molten, seething, boiling, this stuff which had erupted from the center of the earth was the stuff I conceived hell to be made of. We had reached the Boiling Lake.

The gentle, whispery voice just behind me spoke in French to someone else. "A simple matter. The lake has no bottom. Why not dispose of—you understand. Here, afterward?"

Apparently another of my captors understood this

reference, as I did. "No! It is Le Maréchal's decision. If there is to be profit in the whole affair, he must give the order. She is to reach the camp. Is that clear?"

Thank God! My life was to be spared for the moment. No one advised me to walk carefully to avoid that ghastly weapon of nature, the Boiling Lake, but I was able to make out the center of the path and to follow the bare heels of the man in front of me. They were all I could see below my blindfold.

The path spread out into a flat area of dry, packed earth. We must have reached the eastern end of the lake. We followed the lake's edge to the right, the south, I thought. Here, there was activity, another group of men, judging by the confusion of voices. I thought I made out the flicker of a fire and the pleasant scent of wood burning. They all spoke French, rapid and soft, almost unintelligible to one who had learned the deep-pitched, precise French of the court of Versailles. It was all I could do to keep my limbs from trembling as I realized my fate might very shortly be decided. This would be the camp of that man whom most of St. Sebastien followed—Le Maréchal, the black leader.

I was roughly thrust forward by a pair of hands, and I dropped helplessly to my knees. Someone lifted me under my arms, which were still pinioned behind me, and I was furious at myself for groaning at the pain. I could not bear that these treacherous creatures, who perhaps smiled at me by day, should now treat me like a bale of merchandise on the quai. Or like a slave brought to the African coast from the interior.

Among those chattering, eager voices, one voice cut through and made me shudder again, just when I hoped to conquer the wild terror that recurred far too frequently now. The voice was deep and powerful, and made itself heard without effort over those of my talkative abductors.

"What is this? How often must I say it? The whites we attack are male. Do not bring your females to this place. No more! You understand me? No more. This one, for example. Which of you does she belong to?"

I managed to get my voice out, and a difficult thing it was!

"Please! My throat—I am thirsty. My throat!"

The deep, answering voice gave me slight hope, a small release of my anxiety.

"Someone—you, Raoul! A cup there."

A hand, probably that of the chief with the deep voice, put a thick mug to my lips. I took a long swallow and very nearly choked to death. It was not the water I expected but straight rum. While I coughed and sputtered, the chief asked me questions. I could only answer in fits and starts.

"Who are you? You do not belong to one of my men. That much is clear. How did you happen to be taken?"

"I belong—that is, I am Madame Douglas, the—the wife of the Governor of St. Sebastien."

He set his hands on my shoulders and asked my captors, "What does this mean? I have forbidden this kind of thing. It is too unsafe. There are constant witnesses who will end by destroying us."

"But why, master? She is a hostage for his behavior."

"And then, too," someone added, "we can earn a fortune for her. The man cares for her. Anyone can see. We receive the payment. We use it for ammunition. And we destroy these English."

"And have the woman inform her government of every detail afterward? You are a fool!"

One of my original captors, the one with the nasty

plans for me, put in eagerly, "It need not be so, master. The Boiling Lake. Drop her into the Boiling Lake."

I wanted to scream, to offer them all my fortune in London, to confess anything. But my throat was tight and dry and I could make no sound. It was as if a dagger had been thrust, searing hot, through my vocal cords.

I scarcely heard that quiet, authoritative voice as it answered the unspeakable suggestion.

"Very true. A practical solution."

# 12

During the horrible few seconds that followed, one of the men threw twigs and brush on the fire. The wood was naturally damp, and a cloud of smoke engulfed us. Choking, I turned my face away, trying to breathe. The man I took to be Le Maréchal reached for me and helped me away from the campfire.

"It is true we have not yet decided what must be done with you, Madame Douglas, but you will not be harmed until that decision is made. Please be at ease. Aaba, see that the cords are no more uncomfortable than is necessary. Do not concern yourself, madame."

I had barely enough spirit to tell him, in bitterest sarcasm, "Until the moment of your decision, I shall, of course, be completely at ease." I wanted to ask if they would remove this infernal blindfold, but I did not dare to do so. I realized that if I saw any of these men, there would be even less likelihood of my leaving here alive.

Whoever rearranged the cord that bound my wrists did not improve matters, but my object must be to keep from antagonizing these rebels. There were other captives who suffered inconvenience as I did: I heard the whinny of the nervous, protesting horses who had been stolen from the Government House carriage. One of the men called out that if the poor beasts were not quiet they would be eaten. This seemed to strike the band as a witticism, and they all laughed, but I suspected that the animals were bothered by the insects that infested the swamp, as well as by the bats that stayed away from the light of the fire but still could be heard flapping over the treetops of the jungle surrounding us.

After a whispered argument about what to do with me while they sent the terms of my release to my husband, I was ushered to a place beyond the campfire and nearer the swamp; for as I sat huddled against the huge trunk of a tree, I could hear the sucking, digesting noises of the choked swamp waters in the night behind me.

Left to myself, I set about trying to squeeze my fingers through the cords that tied my wrists. I clenched and then relaxed the muscles, and the result seemed promising for a brief time, but then I had to stop when my skin became raw. The ground beneath me was still dry, which provided a small comfort, but that, too, threatened to disappear when I became aware, even with my blindfold, that the moon had gone behind the clouds. Soon the first vagrant raindrops heralding a tropic downpour began to sprinkle the campsite and to trickle through the foliage above my head. In turning my head abruptly to avoid the rain, I caught the lower edge of my blindfold on a sharp, dead twig growing from the trunk of the tree. I worked at this for several long minutes, until the homespun material was loose. I did not want to remove the thing entirely—that was too dangerous, and besides, the blindfold would merely be replaced by a more efficient one—but now I could easily remove it if the right moment came. If only I could get my hands free!

I heard heavy footsteps, booted, I thought, approaching me. Then I caught the voice of their leader, deep and sonorous, but a voice that had readily agreed that the best place for me might be the bottom of the Boiling Lake. I thought I glimpsed the gleam of metal—a knife?—beneath my blindfold. I stiffened, and started to scream. But as before, my throat closed, and I felt the sharp, stabbing pain of my soundless cry.

"Do not flinch, madame," Le Maréchal warned me. "You are not to be hurt. Unless we receive no response from Colonel Douglas."

And after they heard? But I did not want them to put my fate into words. As long as it was not spoken, I felt that there was hope.

"What . . . are you doing?"

"Cutting a lock of that lovely hair. You will not miss it, madame. It will soon grow out again." *If I am allowed to live long enough,* I told myself. "How soft it is! You are a woman worth much to the colonel. Let us hope he realizes this before it is too late. Now, your ring."

"I hope it is not too tight," I managed to say hoarsely as he reached behind me.

One of the men beside Le Maréchal giggled. "Easy enough to remove, eh, master? The ring and the finger, eh?"

Le Maréchal's voice was close to my head as he began to prize off my wedding ring. "That is how it has been done many times to women of our own people. By the Spaniards, by the French. Yes, and by your own English, madame." He had the ring in his hand and stood up again. He must be a tall, powerful man, if I could judge by his shoulders.

"Sir, could you tell me, please," I began, hoping at least to find the identity of Luc Monceau's agent on St. Sebastien. "Someone, the agent of your enemies, wants to murder me. But that person' is not serving you and will never serve you. If you give in to the demands of that agent, you will find yourselves in his power and that of his masters. Surely, you don't intend to give aid to your enemies." It was, in part, a lie; the French agent would probably help them, at least as long as it served his own purpose.

Several voices cut in, disagreeing, some telling him not to listen to me, others—thank God! reminding him that the return of the French might be harder to stop than the English.

"At least, master, the English governor has offered to settle our differences. He has met with some of us and he is sincere, I'd swear. You have given him your word that you will meet with him at Esterby Harbour some time soon, and talk of a truce. You can settle the matter of this woman there. It is not far to the east, and we can get back to Boiling Lake if it proves to be a trap."

"Esterby Harbour has too many English sympathizers," someone objected, and other voices were raised in agreement.

"But it is close," one man repeated. "Le Maréchal could return here in an hour, and the soldiers would not dare to follow. Others, maybe. But not the soldiers. They know what we do to them." He made some sort of gesture, grisly, I am sure, and several of the men laughed.

"I have heard you speak the name of Le Maréchal. My husband speaks of your leader often and with respect," I lied, but I felt it was not a great lie. I knew Ian was interested in a fair peace pact with these people. "This other agent, the French agent, is a betrayer. His master in London wants me destroyed because I know his identity. That is why he offered to pay your men if they murdered me. Do you understand?"

The man I took to be Le Maréchal agreed. "All this may be very true, but it is to our advantage when the French and English are enemies. In this way, we shall win our independence like the Haitians."

"Why not rescue me then?" I asked. "My husband will be eternally grateful, and your cause will—" I didn't finish. Too many furious voices intervened.

In the end it was useless. Le Maréchal set himself to calm these noisy factions, and I was left alone. I worked on my hands until I was sweating, a clammy, icy sweat, and the flesh of my wrists was gone, but I felt no pain, only the spurts of yielding in the cord. An enormous reward. I had never dreamed that so paltry a result could mean this much. The cord was either loosening, or wearing away, or expanding. Whatever it was, I could feel my fingers slip, wriggle and move until my left hand was free. I tore off the dangling cord and cautiously raised the blindfold.

For a minute I was nearly blind. Distant lights, storm lanterns, a torch, the fire sputtering in the rain—all appeared as blurs before I could make out anything clearly. Then I saw Le Maréchal's rebels, scattered over the clearing and beyond, amid the huge foliage. There were more of them than I had suspected. Still, they all appeared to be busy—talking, whittling various objects, and sheltering the fire in a losing battle with the steadily increasing rainfall.

The rain might help me. I considered next what I had heard them say about Esterby Harbour where the residents' sympathies were with the English. And it was only about an hour's walk eastward from Boiling Lake. I studied the sky. A poor time to speculate on directions. The rain was heavier now, falling like a veil between my captors and me. Once my eyes had become used to the night scene, I fancied I could make out the figure of every member of the group, beginning at one end of the camp, far to my left, and completing the semicircle on my right. Until I knew exactly where they all were located, I did not want to risk an escape. I had no doubt that if I were recaptured, there would be no chance whatever of my survival.

A diversion. I needed a diversion that would panic the men or at least send them all scrambling around. There were some women among the groups, and already a quarrel had sprung up over one of them, but this soon ended in a single exchange of blows, one of which missed its target, and the winner pulled his prize off into the heavy foliage that masked the swamp. Some other pretext must serve, then. If there were enough men bobbing around the clearing, all those silhouettes and shadows hopelessly mingled, I would have my chance: I would be just one more silhouette or shadow. And from my position at the west end of the clearing, just inside the skirt of the jungle, I saw that there was a perfect diversion in the making.

One of the rebels, a powerful young man whose bare chest and shoulders gleamed in the firelight, arrived at the edge of the little fire pit with a huge pile of brushwood. I held my breath. All my tired muscles stiffened. I shifted my body slowly, readying my legs so that I might rise to my feet at an instant's notice.

I knew that Le Maréchal had sent one of his men on his way in a westerly direction through the swamp. This must be the man who was carrying my ring and a lock of my hair to my husband. What would Ian Douglas do? He did not love me. Indeed, he scarcely knew me. And he suspected me of varied misbehavior.

I didn't know why he mistrusted me, but there was always the possibility that he would not consider me worth rescuing. I, on the other hand, was immensely attracted to him. It wasn't a very romantic conclusion, and I might not have time left in my life to change his feelings about me. This realization caused me almost as much anguish as the thought of my probable fate. But it reinforced my courage, my determination to escape.

Now the young man with the brushwood was reaching out his arms to drop his load at the same time that one of the older men, thin to the point of emaciation, shouted a warning. Too late, the brushwood fell onto the sputtering wood along with a new downpour of rain. My muscles tensed, and I started to rise at the same time that a great cloud of steam covered the clearing, along with sputtering, hissing noises as the damp wood seemed to explode in the war between fire and water. The worst of it lasted less than a minute, but while they all ran about, throwing dirt on the fire that spattered over the edge of the little pit, and trying to protect what remained of the campfire itself, I stole into the concealment of the jungle.

I thanked heaven that I had been on the east side of the clearing, the side whose trail led toward Esterby Harbour. I took care not to run; my footing was far too precarious, for the ground was riddled with rivulets clogged by the debris of the swamp and innumerable wild, unseen creatures. The tropic downpour struck the great leaves overhead, dripping off the fern fronds so that I was soaking wet in no time, but I made my way in the direction closely paralleling the trail, trying not to lose myself in the jungle. I could see occasional snatches of the sky, especially in the east where it seemed to be clearing. The storm was moving northward toward Mourne Swamp where I had visited that morning.

I reached what appeared to be a more heavily traveled path, obviously near a settlement. I could only pray it would be Esterby. I was able to run for the first time, although even the center of the track was now a muddy runnel. I removed my slipper, stepped with my stockinged foot into the mud, and then put my foot, mud and all, back into the slipper and went on, keeping as close to the jungle growth as possible.

A sudden squall pelted my face in spite of the hood, but it did not stop me, and I was sure the storm was letting up. The horror I had escaped still overwhelmed me; I had scarcely had time to wonder if I were being followed. Or rather, how far behind me my pursuers might be. Movements ahead of me, appearing like skeletal fingers to my terrified imagination, became broken fern fronds blown across my path. Discovering the absurdity of these fantasies, I rushed on, but tree limbs snapped in my face, threatening to blind me. Still, reason had won out in my wild flight through the fern forest, and now I became too confident.

By this time my husband must have reached Government House and gotten the message about my capture. Was it a trap for him? If he came blundering into the jungle after me—and after Le Maréchal, of course—they would have him at their mercy. I was sickened by the thought of his danger—an unnecessary danger, I assured myself with that new excess of confidence, for I had escaped.

I must have covered a considerable distance, I thought, by the time the storm moved on, reduced to annoying trickles and spatters as I hurried along under the giant plants. So suddenly had the storm passed that I heard behind me for the first time the snap and crash of a rotten log overturned by some fast-moving creature. Barely in time, I darted into a copse of low brush and jungle flowers and made my way more slowly, taking care not to betray my whereabouts by a sound that would echo over the noise of dripping water. But I soon found myself in swamp waters. I heard my pursuer's bare feet pounding across the path and into the water behind me, and turned to see a half-naked man, one of Le Maréchal's rebels who had marked my escape and followed me.

I twisted and writhed through the morass, my cloak tightly wrapped around my body as protection against the endless twigs and thorns. The water was alive with small creatures, and I dared not look down. Their chilly, wet bodies briefly touched me, then slipped past. I knew my pursuer was catching up with me, and now he extended a wet, clawlike hand. As I pulled away, tearing the hood off my head, a wild, agonized scream pierced the jungle growth. The native's hand fell away from me. Some creature slithering through those waters had attacked his bare legs.

I rushed out onto the path, never looking back. Although it was still dark, with only a vague light from where the clouds parted and the dawn formed a silver rim on the eastern horizon, I could make out the distant silhouette of a village with the harbor beyond. Several sailing vessels were anchored in the bay, but few fishing vessels or native piraguas. There were heavy breakers beating toward the shore. I had reached the Atlantic coast of the island. I was coming into Esterby.

The village looked desolate, with scarcely a light in any of the little whitewashed houses, and the old French fort, fallen into disuse, was crumbling away.

But I saw lights in the main street, just this side of the long, high wall built to hold off the windward tides of the Atlantic. Here torches flared, illuminating the silhouettes of several figures. I called to them, waving, stumbling forward.

"Help me . . . please!"

A man who appeared to be a sailor loped toward me, bellowing, "Easy, lass! Easy there!" He took one of my arms. "What in tarnation? You came through the swamp, ma'am?" He was joined by a comrade, both of whom spoke English with an extraordinary twang that I couldn't locate until I decided that he came from one of the ships anchored in the harbor, a trading vessel from the United States. As the Yankees usually banded together with the French against the English, I had no doubt that this Yankee ship dealt in contraband, and was one of Le Maréchal's suppliers. But no matter. Every English squire on the Sussex coast likewise traded with the smugglers. When I saw ahead of me a man in the uniform of my husband's regiment, I was overjoyed, and finding new breath and courage, I ran on—only to be seized by his thin fingers and stopped just as I recognized him. He was Lieutenant Felipe.

"Ah! My good fortune, madame. Do not struggle so. How do you happen to be here so pleasantly in my arms?"

I had escaped Le Maréchal only to fall into the hands of this man who had confessed to Agnes Mabberly that he, too, was one of the rebels.

"Abducted!" I managed to get out. I was still breathless and shaking from my remembered terror. "My husband . . . coming for me," I added, hoping thus to forestall any attempt he might make upon my life. At least I had sense enough not to accuse Le Maréchal's men in Felipe's presence.

"But you are in no condition to return yet, madame. It would require a ride halfway around the island. Besides, the governor at this minute may be in Mourne Swamp, pursuing the wandering sailor from the *Maud Vester*. Someone reported his presence to the governor. Meanwhile—"

I managed to wrench myself from Lieutenant Felipe's grasp and ran on to another Yankee sailor, a long-legged figure who was sauntering up the slope from the center of town.

"What's this, ma'am? You Frenchies are the politest folk!"

"No, sir. I am the wife of the Governor of St. Sebastien. Can you get me back to Port Fleur? It is vitally important. The governor may try to enter that ghastly swamp to reach me. People may be killed." Unless, of course, Ian had found the injured sailor, Peter Phipps, and by now had been told the truth about my past as a French agent. In that event a man of Ian's character would not hesitate to make me pay for my treason. I shivered, and the man patted my shoulder reassuringly.

"Sure, ma'am, sure. We'll ask one of your husband's officers here, Lieutenant Felipe."

"No!"

The poor man looked so surprised at my vehemence that, in other circumstances, I would have laughed.

"But ma'am! He is the good governor's man. The very one who'll bring you back to the colonel."

"No. You don't understand. I'll go myself then." But I was so tired, so unspeakably tired. "And—a body—in the swamp there—behind me. A native man attacked by a snake, I think."

The young man put his arm around me. "Here, ma'am. Don't faint now. Don't you faint." Others of his friends seemed to have disappeared, perhaps to search for the injured native.

How could I get home to my husband? Even if I escaped Lieutenant Felipe, how could I prevent Ian from learning the truth about me? I would lose him and my life. It was hopeless. The sailor's panicked voice was far away. As for me, I felt as though I were floating. Noises buzzed in my head, I was aware of my pulsebeat, of my blood pounding, all combining to warn me that I was near unconsciousness. My throat burned so that I could scarcely swallow. The fierce pain in my throat was due in part to my harrowing experiences. To that, yes, but to what else? I held tightly to the sailor's arm and watched as his comrades, assisted by Lieutenant Felipe, brought the body of my pursuer out of the swamp trail. I saw now that he was the man who had brought the firewood to the campfire at Boiling Lake. He appeared to be dead.

"What'll be his ailment?" my Yankee rescuer asked.

The group moved past me, and I saw that one of the black rebel's arms dragged pitifully, like boneless flesh.

One of the sailors answered vaguely. "I tried a shot at the thing, ma'am, but I missed. A snake, just as you thought. The swamp's full of 'em, most likely. And this poor devil . . . with naked limbs."

Lieutenant Felipe looked at me. His teeth were bright in the first light of dawn.

"A fer-de-lance," he explained with horrid, flat simplicity. "We have them occasionally on St. Sebastien. You are fortunate the creature did not attack you. Come, Madame Douglas, let me escort you to Government House."

While I was making vague but no less desperate protests, Lieutenant Felipe drew me on into the town where the dawn's light had brought forth the street sweeper with his long stick and curved broom straws, just as in Paris. And two vultures had swooped down to clean the streets. Steam rose from the rain-washed rooftops. The long night had almost ended, and it was going to be a hot, muggy day.

Not quite ended, though. There was still the matter of Lieutenant Felipe.

"I am too tired to go on," I protested, grasping at anything to keep from being sent off with the lieutenant. "I am soaking wet. I must remain here. Send word to my husband."

How odiously soothing was Lieutenant Felipe! He positively fluttered in his anxiety to get me on my way, and in his company alone. He must know that I would betray all my knowledge of Le Maréchal's camp to the governor.

"Madame's anxiety is understandable. It is a shocking business. While you, our gallant Yankee friends, care for the body of this unfortunate fellow, I will escort Madame the Governor's Lady to her husband."

Never had I heard such deceptively solicitous tones. My only desire at that instant was to find a couch, the ground, anything on which to lie down and sleep, and not to dream about the Boiling Lake and what might have remained of my body in its ghastly depths, nor about my wanderings through the swamp where I had evaded a deadly fer-de-lance but my pursuer had not.

"I intend to remain here at an inn until my clothing is dry," I told Lieutenant Felipe. "I expect to have a hip bath and to rest until my husband comes for me."

But would he come for me—ever? Please let him still care about my fate. Let him come for me before it was too late. Above all, I prayed that he would believe in me.

Over my head I saw the lieutenant and my rescuing Yankee friend exchange glances, Felipe with an expression regretful but noble. He was going to escort the governor's wife even if she were mad enough to shun his company.

"I insist on staying here," I said. But I suspected from the little byplay between the two men that these Americans were somehow in his debt. Certainly they listened to him. And then I realized that it was probably he, as Le Maréchal's agent, who had been sent here to supervise the arrival of contraband from the Yankee ship as well as to sell contraband leaving St. Sebastien. In every way he was a betrayer of my husband. But how much did he know about me? And even with all that I had discovered, how much could I tell Ian Douglas? I knew that to protect my husband and his mission here, I would ultimately have to tell him everything, even about myself. He must learn about the betrayal of his trusted man, and if I told him that, the rest must also follow.

"Well, then," Lieutenant Felipe agreed to my surprise. "Let us stop by the local tavern, borrow some rogue's cloak, and wrap you securely in it. It is true, you are shivering."

I allowed myself to be escorted down the main street to the tavern, where a scullery maid was throwing out the night's slop into the alley. I was helped into a small private parlor behind the taproom, and there, borrowing a homespun gown, a cloak, and shoes from the tapster's wife, I felt freed at last from the mud-encrusted, icy clothing that I had worn as a prisoner at Boiling Lake.

Lieutenant Felipe spoke to the tapster while I was being dressed. Although he talked in low tones, I heard him assuring the tapster that my reluctance to go with him was due to a lover's quarrel with my new husband.

"Tut," said the tapster. "As a new bride, she should be with the governor. You ready yourself. I shall get a noggin of rum down her gullet and she'll go anywhere right enough. You'll see."

If I ever saw Ian Douglas again, I swore firmly to myself, I would tell him the truth. He deserved to know. He wouldn't forgive me, but I must tell him, and if he should, by some marvelous chance, forgive . . .

Back in the taproom, I tried to catch the eye of the tapster, to make him understand that I wanted his help. Then I reached out my hand, but he misunderstood, and offered me a mug of rum diluted with water so hot that it steamed as it approached my lips. I thought for a minute that he and Lieutenant Felipe would force the liquor down my throat, but when they put it into my hands I drank a little. It seemed to help me, but I loathed the thick, sweet taste. After a few swallows I gave the chipped mug to the tapster's wife, unable to force down any more.

"Will you please help me?" I begged her. "I don't want to leave now. Not with—" Lieutenant Felipe looked at me as though with the hooded eyes of a serpent. The tapster's wife soothed, "You will soon be home, ma'am. Do not be afraid."

I found myself escorted outside with many assurances that an immediate return home was in my best interests. A saddled horse waited, and the lieutenant's eyes glittered as he reached out to lift me up. His faint, twisted smile gave the lie to his words as he promised the tapster and his wife, "The lady will be delivered safely to my leader. Be at ease."

"Your leader!" I tried to avoid him. "Let me borrow a second horse. I am strong enough to ride back."

"I am hurt," the lieutenant mocked me. "Madame knows very well how far she can trust me. Who knows better? Come!" His voice hardened. He left little doubt that he was running out of patience. He took my hands when I protested, furious and scared at the compliance of the others, and then I heard the most welcome sound in the world—approaching hoofbeats, and then my husband's stern, quick-tempered challenge.

"What the devil is all this?"

I jerked free and ran to my husband, whose horse, alarmed at his rider's angry voice, suddenly reared up, almost bringing his forelegs down upon my head—in which case he would have carried out what I had no doubt was Lieutenant Felipe's purpose, my death. For all Ian's furious anger, I was so glad to see him that his dark scowl was my greatest joy. When he had swung off the skittish stallion, I ran into his arms, babbling about how glad I was, and he laughed even as he hugged me to him.

"What in God's name are you doing here at Esterby? I thought I had left you safely home in Government House."

By his manner I knew he could not have heard the secret of my past from the wounded sailor. I think he even surprised himself when his rough hand caressed my hair. Over my head he spoke to Lieutenant Felipe.

"Lieutenant, how did you happen to meet my wife here? I thought you were in the interior, searching for Le Maréchal's hideaway."

"I am afraid the information was inaccurate. Your

lady here tells me that she was held prisoner at Boiling Lake. But their camp never remains in one place, and I am afraid it would cost us our lives to go as far as Boiling Lake without a truce. The jungles must be honeycombed with his men."

I explained briefly about the false message and my capture. Ian's arms enclosed me more tightly, but he said nothing except to thank Lieutenant Felipe.

"Lucky she ran into you. This business will go into my reports on the affair. As for me, I had word there was smuggling going on here this morning. I suppose there is nothing for it but to arrest a few of those poor devils who follow Le Maréchal, make examples, and silence the War Office, not to mention the excisemen. Can you take my wife back to Government House?"

"Nothing would give me greater pleasure," Lieutenant Felipe said. He glanced at me and smiled.

# 13

It was the final blow in a night filled with horrors. But I was saved from Lieutenant Felipe's hands after all, because in the midst of my protest I fainted. I remember nothing more until I was lifted off my husband's horse and carried into Government House, so tightly wrapped in my borrowed cloak that I could scarcely move. But of one thing I was certain: I was in my husband's arms, and I had never known any touch that I desired so much.

He brought me into the reception hall where we were surrounded by the household servants and Tirsa, who looked suddenly very old, very haggard. I felt that I must make some effort to stand on my own feet, and I said as much, but was exceedingly pleased when my husband snapped, "Rubbish! Good God, do you think I'm incapable of carrying my own wife!"

Tired and confused as I was, I delighted in his answer, as in his body so near to mine. He took me up to the bed in my suite and laid me down. I scrambled to sit up, and tried to brush the disheveled hair out of my eyes but, still surprising me, he leaned over the bed and with thumb and forefinger cleared the wisps of hair from my face and looked at me, saying nothing.

I attempted a smile. "You have been so good to me."

I fumbled for his hand which he did not draw

away, although he said roughly, "I never was good to a female in my life. Ask your cousin. Or Felipe. They are the ladies' men."

"All the same, I love you for it."

"I wish that were true," he said cryptically.

While I stared at him, not in the least understanding, he seemed to rebuild that curious barrier that had always stood between us.

"You were not ill-treated? They did not—hurt you?"

"Le Maréchal did not permit it. I hurt myself in escaping. And I think Le Maréchal is sincere."

He was the governor again, saying in a clipped voice, "I never doubted it. All he wants is the entire island. We need it for victualing and watering our fleet. It may be said of both of us that we are sincere. It doesn't help. . . . Why do you clasp your neck like that?"

I hadn't been aware of the gesture. I swallowed and explained, "A sore throat. When I am nervous, it is worse. I've had it since this afternoon."

"But you are better now?"

"Quite well, thank you."

He looked at me for a long moment. "How different you are!"

My eyes opened wider. I sensed a compliment on his lips and did not want to lose it. "Different how?"

He seemed to be buried in memories, in bitter thoughts which would have disturbed me but for his forefinger which stroked my hand in an unconscious gesture that I found most exciting.

"I think I told you once, I was married before. Long ago. A pretty young creature. I had no tact, none of those arts of the dandy. She loathed me, poor soul, shrank when I came near her. I suppose I must have disgusted her with what she called my 'coarse ways.' I never could understand her. She lied to me repeatedly about everything. It is the one unforgivable crime. To find one has anchored one's life, one's affections, to a liar who hides every action!"

I started nervously, my conscience sorely troubled. When would he find he had married another lying female, a woman with a past that could bring disgrace and shame to him, and a hangman's noose to my neck. "What—happened to her?" I finally managed.

He drew me to him as though demonstrating the difference between me and that first deceiving wife. "She finally ran off with a powder-and-patches oaf she met at a ridotto. They died in the sinking of the channel packet off the French coast."

"How terrible!"

He nodded, still gazing at my hand. "I thought so. I blamed myself for a while, though I'll confess I got over that idea many a year ago. I knew Agnes somewhere along that time. We occasionally found each other a great consolation. But after ten years, I have the right to forget my first marriage failure, don't you think?"

I raised his finger to my lips. My eyes never left his face, as if they might memorize it, for I knew that the secret of my own guilt made my time with him borrowed at best. When he read in my gesture the depth of my feeling for him, he hesitated a moment, then lowered his head, still watching me. When our lips brushed, even before we kissed, I was shaken by my own violent and joyous reaction. I welcomed him, and he was man enough to sense the reality of my feelings.

Satisfied, he drew away from me and smiled. The harsh lines around his mouth faded. He stepped back, away from the bed. He looked around and saw Pepine and Darielle. "Take good care of Madame. And see if you can discover why her throat troubles her."

He was gone then, and he and I still had not really talked. He always made that impossible.

While the rest of St. Sebastien was enjoying breakfast, I soaked in a hip bath brought into my bedchamber. I tried to find the words to tell my husband the truth about myself, my reason for coming to St. Sebastien and for accepting his proposal. But I would lose him forever. For his feelings about me were rooted deep in his past bitterness.

For a few minutes I had almost hoped Ian knew of my past, of Luc Monceau. Then the terrible dread would be over, and there might be some hope for our future together.

When Darielle and Pepine insisted on helping me to dress, Darielle was full of questions but the other girl, I noted, was extraordinarily quiet.

Darielle giggled happily. "What an adventure, madame! Colonel Douglas was gone when the messenger from Le Maréchal arrived. We did not know his news, and the man waited such a time! And at last he left the message and the little packet and went away."

"Has my husband seen the message yet?"

"Yes, he has just seen it, and such a look! He loves Madame. One could not doubt it."

I hoped it might be true. What a rich life we would have if only there were no secrets between us! Meanwhile, there was his trust in Lieutenant Felipe that grew more dangerous every hour. The man could betray Ian and his small British contingent at any time. I had to warn my husband, no matter what happened, or how much Lieutenant Felipe told him about me.

I hoped that once I had bathed away my aches and pains, and my wrists were cleanly wrapped, I would also have washed away the annoying pain in my throat that stabbed at me persistently. It was not to be, however. I could scarcely swallow a bite when Darielle brought me toast and fruit. Even the tea was an effort.

"It is very strange," the girl murmured thoughtfully, shaking her head. "We should perhaps ask in the kitchen what is the trouble."

"My nerves, probably. I thought for quite some time last night that I would be drowned in the Boiling Lake. When I close my eyes I can feel the blindfold and the cords on my wrists."

She gave a little gasp. "Your wrists, madame! The flesh was gone! How they must pain you!"

"Not so much now. My thanks to you and Pepine. No, it is my throat—I can scarcely swallow."

"You have a disease, you think?"

"No. Nothing like that. It is simply that I am a prey to nerves. So much has happened since I broke with Luc—" Horrified at my own carelessness, I corrected myself, "since I left the ship."

Darielle accepted my correction without even a blink, but Pepine raised her head. Her dark liquid eyes stared at me. I wondered, not for the first time, if Pepine had some relationship with Le Maréchal's men.

In spite of Darielle's shocked protests, I left my bedchamber and made my way down to my husband's study. In the lower hall I came upon Tirsa moving away from the salon which led to the governor's study. Had she been listening at a keyhole? It would not surprise me.

Still looking stiff and frightened, she touched her lips with the tip of her tongue and said with a ghastly effort at cheerfulness, "It is good to see you up and about, madame. We understood you were in great danger of drowning in one of our swamps. You should take care."

"It was not of my own doing, I assure you," I said coolly.

I was about to pass her, but she persisted.

"Madame, I did not trust Lieutenant Aaba's message. I told Lieutenant Felipe. He—he said he would find you. The governor says he did help you. This is true, is it not? It was Lieutenant Felipe who saved you?"

Why had Lieutenant Felipe not told me he came to rescue me? Why should he make me believe he was worse than he was? I could not believe his motive had been noble.

"I am happy to say I saved myself," I snapped.

"But Lieutenant Felipe—"

"You may be sure Lieutenant Felipe intended to do a great deal. He did not have the opportunity, however."

I had not satisfied her, but I hurried into the little salon outside my husband's study. My knees were trembling against the muslin of my skirts, and I had to grasp the draperies at the open window while I stood waiting for Ian to complete his business with the visitor in his study. He certainly needed an adjutant, or at least a secretary, to handle his business, but knowing Ian as I was beginning to, I realized he liked to do everything himself.

I was beginning to distinguish the voices in the study now. I heard an exclamation from my Cousin George, who was receiving the details of my misadventure. I thought I recognized Agnes Mabberly's voice. My throat troubled me so much now, that I rested my forehead against the window frame as I stared at the sapphire-blue waters of the bay. They looked clean and cool. How long ago it seemed since I had opened one of the windows upstairs so that George might throw out the silly little voodoo doll he had found in his napkin.

I thought of the voodoo doll with the bodkin piercing its neck. I rubbed my throat. No. Impossible. I was not superstitious. The doll was gone, lying at the bottom of the bay . . . but with the bodkin still stabbing through its throat? I wished suddenly that I had removed it before I had cast the doll away into the water.

The door of my husband's study opened. I started forward, and Agnes started to leave but hesitated.

"My girls and I will bury the man, since we have cared for him during his—illness."

My husband's voice sounded then, ironic, unsympathetic. "Nevertheless, I was not informed of the importance of this sailor."

"You were busy, sir. You were in pursuit of Le Maréchal, but we left the message with your—"

I stiffened, stood stock still outside the door, feeling as though I waited for the death thrust. She went on after a second's pause, "—with your staff."

"And this Phipps is dead without making a confession. I don't like it. Now we shall never know why he deliberately dropped those rifles—if it *was* deliberate. Captain Hollin and my men think he was a French agent."

"Or a Yankee," Agnes suggested, and I wondered if what she said could be true. "He may have been trying to escape from the island on one of those Yankee vessels. He must have known he couldn't escape on a British ship."

"Yes, those damned Yanks are no friends of ours," my husband agreed.

"Well, it won't be necessary for you to handle the case now. We will bury him quietly. If one of your men hadn't seen his body the entire affair would be forgotten by now."

"Very well," Ian said. "The burial within twenty-four hours. We don't dare to leave them longer in this climate. I'll come by and give the permission before morning. Or Captain Adare can do so. I've got to go into the jungle after our old friend Le Maréchal to-night. This assault on my wife is the last straw. I don't care if they all worship him, if he thinks he is Bonaparte himself! He cannot abduct my wife and expect to be considered an honorable foe."

"Now, see here, old man," George put in, ruffled for the first time. "I love my cousin, too. I consider it a personal duty to join in cleaning out that area around Boiling Lake."

"You may love your cousin, but I am her husband. I am going to find Le Maréchal. There will be no more sanctuary if our plans work out tonight. I leave the minute Felipe returns from Esterby to lead the second expedition. If you really wish to help, George, you will see that my wife is protected tonight."

Agnes Mabberly walked out into the salon, but stopped when she saw me. She was very pale, and the sight of me did not help to calm her.

"You!" She came closer. "Miss Adare, you'll not be telling them that Lieutenant Felipe visited Phipps. In fact, we must not say anything about him in connection with that affair. Le Maréchal's men would massacre us all."

I started to say something, but she cut me off with a wave of her hand. Ian Douglas had come to the doorway.

"Madeline! What are you doing out of bed? You

shouldn't be standing out there. George, bring a chair. Good day, Agnes. Captain Adare will attend to the problem of forms and whatnot for the dead man." She turned away, dismissed. "Madeline, I thought I made it clear you were to rest."

He was escorting me into his study where Cousin George shoved a chair under me. George's stream of concerned chatter made me want to laugh, but at the same time I hoped he would leave us alone; Ian's surprising tenderness made me hope this might be the one time when I could reach him with my confession.

Cousin George looked from me to my husband. "I know you two have your little secrets from an outsider. Suppose I bow my way out. By the bye, I suspect the Yankee trader that anchored off Port Fleur last week and was refused admission to the port is the very one delivering contraband at Esterby. I could busy myself on that. I won't need more than a pair of loyal lads for the job."

"First, you will find out anything you can about the dead sailor, that is to say, why our men did not go into the swamp and capture him earlier when they wounded him."

George's eyes widened. "B-but I say, it would have been worth their lives to go into that swamp. Besides, he would have died anyway from one of the swamp creatures if not of his wounds, if—"

"Yes. *If!* But he was saved, by one of Mabberly's females. And George—don't go dashing off after Agnes tonight. I saw the way you looked at her, but I need you here, with my wife."

George grinned, saluted both of us, and left in the wake of Agnes Mabberly. In view of the threats Lieutenant Felipe had made, she might have reason to be afraid. None of us knew whom we could trust in this town. Some of Agnes's own servants might be in the pay of Le Maréchal.

Ian sat down on a corner of his desk and looked at me.

"Now, tell me why you disobeyed me." He pretended a scowling severity, but this time I saw through it and gave him the most blinding smile of which I was capable.

"We see so little of each other, sir, that I thought I should make the effort. And if you please, let us not quarrel this time."

I lifted my hands beseechingly, in deliberate exaggeration, so that he would recognize my sincere attempt at peacemaking, and return my smile. He did not smile, but I thought his mouth appeared less rigid. That was promising. I went on.

"You are apparently under some delusion about me. Would you very much mind telling me why you behave so oddly? A short time ago I thought you liked me. Now, you are your old, untrusting self. You don't know me well enough to dislike me so much."

This time he did smile, not quite as I had hoped, however.

"Why did you agree to marry a man you did not know? A beautiful woman of the quality. A woman with a fortune of her own. Come now, my devoted Madeline, why?"

I should have been afraid of him but for my feeling that he was anxious—as anxious as I.

"Why? But you seem to know the answer. Or what you conceive to be the answer."

He had taken one of my hands again. Curiously enough, even the touch of his callused palm was exciting to me. If only I could have met him earlier, before there were so many ugly secrets in my life. . . .

As if changing the subject, he said thoughtfully, "I have the ring that belongs on this finger. The packet was left with Tirsa, along with orders to me. The instructions as to precisely what would happen to my lovely wife if I did not yield in every way to that rebel's demands."

"They also took a few strands of my hair."

Was it possible that this tough, masterful man could blush? And yet, it seemed to me that his face reddened at my reminder.

"So they did. I thought you might have forgotten. I rather hoped you had." He dropped my hand, to my regret, and reached for the snuff box on his desk. Opening the delicate French mechanism, he showed its contents to me. There in the otherwise empty little case was a curl of my hair. I was so touched that tears sprang to my eyes. He must have been reassured by that, for he set the snuff box back, and taking my ring from his waistcoat pocket, slipped it on my finger.

"Shall we begin again, Madeline? Give me my chance, and I swear you will forget he exists."

*Luc Monceau?* Did he know about my enemy? I prayed that this was true and that he had forgiven me.

"Who exists?"

"Damn it! I wish you would be honest with me. I've known from the beginning why you married me. It was that lover you had in London. Married, I presume. The one you ran away from."

"What!" My head whirled. I hadn't the least notion what he was talking about.

"Your cousin George told me. Said you were running away from an unhappy love affair. Obviously the fellow was married."

"No! Oh, no!" It was all my fault, after all. I had

told George almost that very thing to explain why I must leave London in such haste. I looked up.

"Ian, I have never been in love before. Not with any man in London, married or single. Nor with anyone else. I told George that tale because I had come to hate London. I was alone. My parents were dead. And your proposal sounded romantic. As, indeed, it was."

"Me? Romantic? Good God!" His laughter was delightful, boyish and genuine. How different from the affected laughter of the Prince of Wales's Carlton House set in London!

"I find you exceedingly romantic, my husband," I insisted. I stood up to prove it, kissing him lightly, jokingly, upon the cheek while my fingers brushed his lips.

He watched all this, withstood my endeavors, and then, as I began to withdraw, wondering if I had read his emotions incorrectly, he imprisoned my hands, locked them behind me, and pulled me against his body. His embrace was a vise, stifling to me, but my own pulse raced so that he might have smothered me in that embrace and I should not have protested. If this was a simple husbandly kiss, this consuming heat of our union, then I had never been kissed before.

He set me away from him then, still with his hands holding tightly to my arms. "You will never know how I wanted you that night when we were separated by that endless parade of busybodies at the banquet. Did you think of me at all, Madeline? The truth now! I hate lies."

"I don't know if I loved you then. I certainly wanted you."

He held me to him again, and I felt his cheek against mine, his powerful body, and I thought I was the luckiest woman alive.

The rattle of the door latch sounded behind us. I was sure we had been seen but was unembarrassed at being caught in my husband's arms. Ian's quick temper was triggered, but at my expression he forced a laugh.

"Tirsa, will you please knock—or at least scratch—on the door after this?"

The housekeeper lowered her eyes as she curtseyed. I wondered what had happened to make her look so unwell. Her presence put me in mind of the serious matter I had neglcted: I must warn Ian about Lieutenant Felipe.

I said, "Would you mind returning in a few minutes, Tirsa? There are still one or two plans the governor and I must make."

He watched me curiously while Tirsa, with obvious reluctance, made another bobbing curtsey and retreated, but left the door ajar. I stepped over to the door, closed it, and returned to Ian. In a voice little above a whisper, which I did not believe she could hear even at a keyhole, I said, "Please do not put too much trust in Lieutenant Felipe. He is in sympathy with Le Maréchal."

His reaction puzzled me. He asked no questions, not even how I came to know this alarming fact. He seemed very calm, although slightly annoyed that I had interfered in men's affairs.

"Now, Madeline, I do not want to hear you discuss Felipe again. Such talk is dangerous." As I looked my astonishment, he added, "Someone may come to believe you. I hope you haven't magnified a personal difference out of proportion. He is one of my best men."

"He is Le Maréchal's man. He is working for the rebels, not for English interests."

"How can you possibly know?" He didn't believe

me. He might love me but he certainly didn't believe in my intelligence, not in any true sense of the word. I was prepared with a lie.

"I heard the rebels speak of him. He is their man."

Ian was silent. Then he sighed and shrugged. "We are getting reinforcements within the month, but with Lieutenant Aaba lost to us after that cold-blooded business involving you last night, I count on Felipe more than ever." He was being singularly obtuse, not at all the strong administrator I had come to know.

"Believe me, Ian," I said as firmly as I knew how. "Think of my advice as coming from someone you trust. A friend. Please assume that what I tell you is the observation of a trained spy. Not a woman. Not your wife."

"But you are my wife." His somber face broke into a sunny grin. "That will be difficult, to picture you as a comrade, or worse, a hired spy. I prefer you as a woman. Now run along and I will get back to work. You are much too distracting to be a governor's wife."

He kissed my cheek, gave me one long look, his eyes never more vivid, more promising, and let me go. How dear to me he was, even if he did believe me addle-pated!

I went out into the salon, where Tirsa waited in the middle of the room, as if determined to satisfy me that she had not been listening at the keyhole. She looked after me.

"Madame, will you have time today to give me my menus for the week?"

I said I would be available at any time, and turned toward the great staircase. It was only as I reached the landing, halfway up, that I felt the exhaustion of the night's terrors and my lack of sleep. I was sustained by my new realization that Ian loved me, or at least desired me as I desired him, but physically I was ready to drop when I reached my bedchamber. How welcome it looked, cool and green, not yet heated by the burning rays of the westerly sun.

I was excessively thirsty, for I had drunk little when the girls brought me breakfast. The throbbing in my throat, and with it the burning sensation, were so intense now that I could scarcely swallow. Yet I knew that I could not be truly ill because I had been barely aware of the pain when I was with Ian.

Darielle came in to turn down the bed and to ask if she might help me in any way. Before I could say anything, she said, "The throat, madame, it troubles you?"

I hadn't realized how much I betrayed my nervous problem by touching my throat.

"Oh, I'm afraid it's becoming a habit. My throat does hurt. It burns and aches."

"An illness of the throat, madame?"

"No. It isn't like that. It seems to be my imagination. I doubt if there is anything really wrong."

Darielle put her fist to her mouth and giggled nervously.

"Maybe the *houngan* has put a curse on you."

I started to lie down upon the bed, which looked so welcome. "Don't be ridiculous. I've never even seen a *houngan*. How could he put a curse on me? And why?"

"To help the rebels, madame. If you are ill, and you go home, maybe the English all will go. But it is not necessary that he see you to do such a wicked thing. Anything that is part of you will do. The hairs of your head, the parings of your nails. A doll made in your likeness."

I sat up. "There was a doll. Yesterday. My cousin found it, but I thought it was meant for me."

Darielle swung around, her eyes searching. She was very nearly in a panic.

"But where, madame? We must find it and remove whatever it is that the *houngan* has put into the throat. Or you will die. You will be strangled."

I tried to be airy about her fears but didn't quite deceive myself. "Well, it's too late now. We threw it into the bay."

I was not comforted by her horrified gasp. She backed away from me as though she found me contaminated by the poison of her witch doctors. Then she got hold of herself, sympathy perhaps warming her to the cause of this woman who, she appeared to think, was in the last extremities.

"It can be recovered? That is the only hope."

# *14*

I laughed at the comical horror of this whole affair. That I, an Englishwoman in this year of 1805, should be pursued by the superstitions of darkest Africa seemed incredible, yet my throat hurt even as I laughed.

"But could it be recovered from the bay?" I asked.

"Where in the bay? Near the shore? Easy to find?" Darielle asked me, still with that glazed look of terror.

"I shouldn't imagine so. We threw it out one of the windows. That one, I think."

She crossed herself, a curious gesture in view of her pagan superstitions, and peered out the open window, looking down as far as she could.

"There is a ledge below, against the stone foundations of Government House. A person with steady limbs might walk along the ledge at low tide. It has been done. But if one slips, one is washed off the ledge. And it is very deep in the bay beyond."

By this time she had me hurrying to the window to share her speculation on the danger of recovering the doll. The stone foundation of Government House plunged straight down at a right angle to the ledge, which was presently covered by the bay waters. It seemed to me quite impossible to recover anything from that ledge, even if the doll had not washed away.

"Never mind, Darielle. I need sleep. That is all. If this is some witch doctor's mumbo-jumbo, then the best cure for it is calm nerves. Would you please draw the curtains and I'll try to recover the sleep I missed last night."

Darielle did as I asked, but before she left the room she stopped beside my bed. At this hour the room was not shadowed, and yet I felt a strange, dark presence even in a person as friendly as Darielle. What did I know of these people? I was an alien in this world, Darielle's world, and although I liked her, I did not wholly trust her any more than she and her people trusted me. Was it even remotely possible that Darielle was right, and that my throat trouble was caused by the long, sharp bodkin thrust into the doll's wooden neck?

What nonsense! If I didn't stop these thoughts, I would become as ridden with superstition as the most primitive member of Le Maréchal's following.

"You will sleep, you think, madame?"

Her voice startled me; she had stood there so still, so serene after her outburst, and now she was staring at me with those large, opaque dark eyes.

"I am certain I shall. Thank you, Darielle."

It was very quiet after Darielle left. I found myself listening for various sounds—the chatter of maids cleaning in the hall, and through the open windows, male voices singing plaintively in the neat little piraguas that dotted the bay. I swallowed hard. I tried to concentrate on these soothing sounds, but a few seconds later I became convinced that I was choking. I sat up in bed, massaging my throat. It was perfectly evident that my trouble was of my own making: last night I had struggled to save my own life, and only half an hour ago I had been lost in my newfound love for my husband.

Now I was alone and had time to think, and I was turning into an absurd, overimaginative creature with an illness that did not actually exist. I lay down again, firmly resolved to sleep. This time I began to hear other sounds—horses on the gravel road, carriage wheels—and I wondered if the Government House carriage and horses had been located and returned from that hideous swamp. Perhaps I had caught some disease while I wandered through the swamp last night. In a sense that would have been the fulfillment of a curse put upon me by one of their *houngans*, their witch doctors.

There had been other moments of fear in my life, and by the furious and determined exertion of my will I overcame those fears. I would overcome this by devoting my thoughts to another and infinitely more important matter, my future relations with my husband. I had never believed I could permit myself to love one man throughout my life. When other men entered my life there was always Father, or Luc Monceau, to remind me that my handsome or appealing suitor had connections with the War Office, or the Admiralty, or was a member of a certain club whose casual gossip would help the French cause.

I slept finally.

But nightmares filled my sleep. The last was the most vivid: I had been found out. My trial was over. The judge, pronouncing sentence, dropped onto his juridical wig the cap of death. I saw the gesture but it did not give me as much pain as the face of my judge. It was that of Ian Douglas, harsh, stern, embittered. Nor was there compassion in that face when he had completed his sentence. And that was a lie, for the real

Ian Douglas would show compassion and regret after his anger. Quick-tempered he might be, but he was not a man for long, secret vindictiveness. He wasn't ruthless like the judge in my dream.

Then I was on the scaffold. I could not recall walking up the wooden slats of the steps. I was simply there, my hands bound behind me. The hangman raised the black hood above my head. I knew that hangman. He was Luc Monceau. I saw the noose dangling high over the black hood.

I was in darkness. That would be the hood. It was hot and stifling. I could scarcely breathe. And then came the touch about my throat like a heavy necklace settling there, and after that touch my throat was enclosed in a vise. Tighter . . . tighter . . . agony to try and draw a breath.

I awoke choking, attempting to scream, but my throat was closed. I could scarcely utter a sound. I had slept for several hours. It was long after noon, and the room was so hot I imagined waves of heat floated through the air. This explained my dream of the ghastly black hood that had stifled me. And the noose? My throat was dry, and the stabbing pain remained.

That damnable doll lying on a shelf of rock so near the base of Government House!

I got out of bed, dizzy at the rapid movement, and reached for the carafe of water. It was no use. I could not swallow. I rang for one of the servants, hoping to have Darielle appear. I was too nervous and in too much discomfort to wait in my room. I went out in the hall in the expectation of meeting her and ran into Pepine.

"I rang for Darielle. Would you please ask—" I could not recognize my own voice, my throat was that raw. I had to begin again in order to make myself understood. At the same time I watched Pepine closely, saw the way her eyes seemed to grow larger, more sharply focused as she stared at my throat. She had heard my voice. She knew what had happened. Very likely, it was she who had put the doll in my napkin on the table, expecting me to eat the luncheon that Cousin George inherited.

"Madame is ill?"

I could have struck her. Odious creature, gloating over another's pain! But then, I despised myself for laying the blame on others when the ultimate guilty party was myself, my own imagination.

"Last night's excursion through the swamp did not improve my health. Where is Darielle? I will find her myself."

She turned hurriedly. "No, madame. I will fetch her up. She is airing bed linens, I believe."

She started away. I called after her that I would meet Darielle out in the shade of the portico, and then I followed Pepine downstairs.

Two men were cleaning the woodwork in the dining room, and the small salon adjoining the governor's study was crowded with people waiting to see Ian. I suddenly remembered what George had said some time ago, that Colonel Douglas was always in difficulties with the War Office because he tried to help those he conquered. I could believe that, and I meant to change myself, to provide a warm, sympathetic home for him during the few hours of each day when he was free of his cares and duties. I had made a bad start in blaming Pepine and Darielle because my own imagination had got the better of me.

I heard running footsteps, bare feet slapping upon the floor of the reception hall. When Darielle met me, breathless and anxious, I motioned her to follow me and stepped off the north end of the portico where, as I had hoped, I found myself beside the foundations of Government House.

"Madame! Your throat, it still troubles you?"

"Very much. Darielle, I know this is absurd, and purely my imagination." It required a tremendous effort even to speak. I knew I was forcing myself to the limit: was it possible my own will could win? "Your *houngan* works on my imagination. Do you understand?"

She shrugged. "But yes. Only you will die if nothing is done. You are here now. The ledge is this way. At the back of Government House. Do you wish that someone goes down into the water and looks for the doll?"

"Can you persuade one of the boys to do this without anyone else finding out what we are about?"

She looked over her shoulder. No one was around. Government House appeared momentarily deserted. Nor was this surprising. I found the air stiffling hot, although the afternoon was well advanced. Darielle leaned toward me confidentially. There was still fright in her manner, but something else warred with this emotion. I wondered if greed was stronger than her fear.

"Madame would pay for this?"

"Yes. Gladly. Can it be done?"

She moved over the embankment, her toes curling into rock and crevice. I followed her carefully, aware of my slippers' smooth soles; a misstep could send me over into the bay, to join the devil doll. Darielle knelt suddenly and peered over the edge of the cliff into the bay below. To our left we could see the west foundation of Government House plunging straight down to the rocky ledge which shelved out into the bay,

"Madame, I have a friend, a freedman like me. We wish to marry. But we must have money for a café. We are saving, but we still need almost six hundred francs. Good francs. Not the Revolutionary French *assignats*. They are worthless. You understand?"

"Perfectly. Can you get this young man to dive? Or—" I could not think clearly. My throat tightened again, constricting against the sharp pain. I tried once more. Firmly. "Or should he take a boat of some kind?" Actually, it seemed to me that the simplest way would be to let myself down onto the ledge and walk its length at the base of the Government House's foundation. But I hoped that I could persuade an expert swimmer to do this instead—someone surefooted, who would not be washed off the ledge which was covered by water even at low tide.

Darielle was not fooled by my firm tone; the hoarseness of my voice told her my problem was critical. As for me, I hated the weakness that my voice betrayed. If I were elsewhere than on this primitive island with its contagious superstitions, I could undoubtedly have cured myself in a matter of minutes. But I was frantic to breathe normally again, and in my panic I would resort to any remedy, even voodoo.

Darielle wriggled her way to the north foundation of the great house. The ledge projected in a westerly direction from the base of this stone foundation. Still kneeling to get a closer view, she motioned me to join her. I did so, finding it less easy to kneel in my tight-skirted gown than Darielle had in her full homespun skirts.

"See?" She pointed downward into the waters, glittering gold on the surface but of an incredible clarity far below. "The doll, it is there. I am sure of it. It has washed back onto the ledge and is caught there. I could reach it if I held onto the wall; but I am much too short, and the water is above waist-deep on the ledge. I would be afraid. I am sorry."

"Perhaps—I can. I am taller. With a rope, something to hold, I could walk along that ledge."

She looked as shocked at the notion of the governor's wife walking in the bay water as she had been at the idea of a witch doctor's curse.

"It is not possible. Ladies do not swim, madame."

But I did. I had swum as a child on visits to the little cove near my father's birthplace in County Mayo. And to be free of this pressure in my throat, to be able to take a long breath without pain, was worth the small physical danger involved. I, too, was certain I could see the wooden doll lodged on the shelf of rock very near the edge, where it fell off sharply into the depths of the bay. I knelt there, looking down.

"Someone may see, madame."

"Go into the carriage house and see if you—if you can find a piece of hemp. A rope. Something."

She scrambled to her feet. "At once, madame."

While she was gone, I asked myself: *Was this really Madeline Mary Adare? This impossible, superstitious creature, panicking at an imaginary ailment?* There was a rock beneath my fingers. In angry frustration, I took it and hurled it out over the cliff's edge. It fell just this side of the ledge and went down, down, how far down I could not even see.

Breathing raggedly, I tried to consider my preposterous problem. It seemed a very small thing, merely to recover a wooden doll and thus drive away the curse that had fallen upon me. What was to keep the witch doctor, the *houngan*—whoever he might be—from sending out another devil doll to curse me? But I could not think of that now. One curse at a time, I thought, and tried to laugh, but that was impossible.

Darielle returned at once, dragging some woven hemp and an old homespun storm cape.

"Simple," she announced. "The rope was under the portico. Fishermen use it to enter the grottoes from above." I felt the hemp, and nodded. It was thin but strongly woven. Abruptly, Darielle's mood changed. She added mournfully, "You will really do this yourself, madame? But what happens now with the francs you promise?"

Too nervous to speak, I nodded vigorously. Absurdly or not, I had now convinced myself that my only cure was the recovery of the doll. I whispered hoarsely, "Can you hold the rope's end?"

"I will tie it here as the fishermen do." She did so, looping the rope around a heavy wooden brace of the building's foundation. "You will not wish to enter Government House in clothing that is soaked, so I have borrowed this cape from the overseer. He is in Port Fleur to buy field slaves. He will not need it."

I had become so desperate in my anxiety and pain that I did not even think about the proprieties. Yet Darielle was right, of course. I could scarcely re-enter Government House dripping wet and half-naked in my shift. Aside from the disgrace to myself, it would humiliate my husband, and this was a poor way to help him.

"Good." Crouched below the house as we were, we might conceivably be spotted by anyone looking out from the west windows, but in such a case, we should see our spy. Anyway, we had gone too far to turn back now.

With Darielle's help I got out of my gown. She eyed me anxiously. "Madame, you breathe with difficulty. Can you do this thing?"

"I must. I need not swim. I need only walk along the ledge. The water will not be over my head." I removed my slippers. In my shift and petticoat and stockings I lowered myself from the cliff's edge to any outcropping I could find, all the while holding tight to the rope. The water was pleasantly cool on this hot afternoon, but the further I immersed myself, the harder it became to breathe. I cursed the St. Sebastien *houngan* a hundred times as I moved along the slippery ledge, pulling the rope with me. It was almost taut now. I thanked heaven the tide was out. A high tide might have washed me off the ledge and the devil doll with me. As it was, the bay surged across the ledge in waves, knocking me against the cliff below Government House. At its peak the water reached nearly to my shoulders but no further. The muscles in my throat tightened. I heard myself cry out but ignored the pain as I sank beneath the water, feeling for the doll. My own movements had shifted the accursed thing.

"Damnation!"

I tried again, groping underwater, and then it was in my fingers. I waved it triumphantly over my head, the first thing Darielle saw as she screamed at me, "The neck! See what is done to the neck!"

Dripping wet, and conscious of a red mist that seemed to rise before my eyes, I rose from the water. With only one free hand, I could scarcely remove the bodkin from the soaked wood, so I applied my teeth to the head of the long pin and drew it out. The exertion did nothing to help my breathing but I managed to keep my balance as I shifted back through the water toward the rock-studded cliff by which I had descended.

I was now only waist-deep. I heard a sharp squeal like a cry that had been stifled, and at the same time the hemp I held suddenly slackened. I looked up. The other end of the rope had been wound in several loops around Lieutenant Felipe's lean wrist. He was staring down at me, with that remembered smile which told me nothing.

I tried to think before I acted, but in my present state of nerves this was not easy.

Darielle begged tearfully, "Please, Monsieur Felipe! Madame must have the rope tied so it will support her. Do not tease. It is dangerous."

With an enormous effort I managed to laugh and wave my hand that held the rope's end. "I was showing Darielle my ring—the one that was returned to me by the rebels. And it slipped out of my hand."

But Lieutenant Felipe stood there watching my absurd predicament, which might indeed become dangerous if he delayed much longer. Without shifting his gaze from me, he gave Darielle a smooth order: "Run along. You are no longer needed."

"No!" I cried in renewed panic. "Darielle—stay!"

She was confused, but instinctively obeyed the male voice, and even as I called her, first pleading, then furious, then anxious, she shrank back from the cliff's edge, and at last ran toward the front of Government House, not daring even to look back.

I tugged at the rope, hoping to ignore his sinister attitude, as I had done in the past. Lieutenant Felipe hefted the rope in his wrist as if weighing the worth of my rescue. Then he turned, apparently to retreat in Darielle's wake. What was going on in his mind? The importance to Le Maréchal if I, who shared Agnes Mabberly's knowledge, were killed?

I now despaired of being rescued by him, and searched for rocks by which I might hoist myself back up the cliff without his help. I thought I might succeed—unless he stood at the top and shoved my groping fingers off the edge with one of his fashionable British boots.

I had no idea what he might do next as my shaking fingers reached for the rock above me, but we were both startled by the thunderous voice of the man who had saved me once before: my hot-tempered husband.

"What in the name of all the devils in hell are you doing, Felipe!"

He had thrown open the window of his study and was staring down at us. Lieutenant Felipe got a sudden grip on the rope, taking in the slack, and I felt the hard pull on my arm.

"Madame fell into the bay, Colonel," he explained smoothly.

My throat did not seem to be improving as rapidly as I had hoped, but I called up to Ian, "I lost my ring!"

Ian looked over my totally improper garments, or what he could see of them above the waterline. He was wide-eyed—with shock, I imagined. The next instant he disappeared from the window. Guessing what would come next, I called to Lieutenant Felipe, "I suggest you leave now, Lieutenant. Don't make this— belated attempt to save me. It won't be appreciated by my husband."

He must have understood that I was referring in part to my state of *deshabille*. His superior officer would not appreciate the lieutenant's seeing me only half-clothed. He looped the hemp around an outcropping of heavy rock, and after saluting me ironically, spun around and strode away. I could have climbed up with a little exertion now, but decided to wait for my husband to rescue me. I was certain he would prefer it.

At that moment I heard a window being closed on the upper floor of the house. I peered up again, and it seemed to me that I had glimpsed Tirsa's sad, proud face. But she was no longer at the window.

Darielle must have remained somewhere close by, because she came running back to the cliff's edge, calling, "Be easy, madame. He will come soon." She seemed very close above me. "The throat, madame? It is relieved, no?"

"No!" I cried hoarsely. "Fetch me that cape. I cannot let the governor's visitors see me like this."

Comprehension dawned. She reached around for the cape which apparently lay in a heap on the cliff's edge. She took the bundle and started to hurl it over the side at me, but as I was still waist-deep in water, I had to scream at her to stop. At least my voice was beginning to sound more human, more natural. I must have taken several breaths before I realized that I was doing so. I thanked God for that and for the relaxing of the sharp pain in my throat . . . but how horrible to reflect that all this suffering was the result of a witch doctor's curse!

When this dreadful day was over, I felt I would regard it as both the best and the worst day of my life. I had come to know Ian Douglas, to know I could love him more than anyone I had ever met. And surely, he loved me a little. But today had also opened my eyes to my weaknesses. That I, Madeline Adare, a woman who had lived her own life for three years, scorning the disapproval of London society, should actually permit herself to be ruled by a *houngan*—it was past belief!

Above me Darielle gasped suddenly, "Oh, monsieur! She is here. Safe, monsieur."

Seconds later my husband was standing on the cliff's edge. He reached for my hands. He looked both angry and concerned. He could not quite touch me, and went down on his knees to try again. Then my groping fingers were caught in his hands. I felt myself swung out over space, but in his hands I knew myself to be secure. Nevertheless, I was remarkably relieved when my stockinged feet touched the ground. With his hands now enclosing my wrists, he instructed Darielle, "Throw that . . . cape, whatever it is, about my wife."

"I am so sorry. I never meant anyone to know," I murmured. I gazed up at him, trying to demonstrate my feeling for him and my regret at embarrassing him, with my eyes. He bundled me into the overseer's cape and then, as I continued to look at him, he bent his head, and to the astonishment of the nervous Darielle, he kissed me, disgracefully dripping though I was. I clung to him, and in that moment I was so happy that I forgot the past, forgot the fears that had racked me, even the *houngan* whose doll had sent me into such hysteria.

Darielle cleared her throat presently, arousing us to the absurdity of our situation. Ian, or his kiss, had lifted me to my toes. He set me down gently and Darielle forced my slippers on over my wet stockings.

"Damn!" Ian said, startling both the maid and me.

"I know I should never have done it—" I began, but he waved aside my renewed apology.

"Of course, it was stupid, my darling, but at least it makes you human. I was beginning to think, after your peerless behavior last night, that you were too perfect!"

"Too perfect!" The awful irony of it made me cringe.

He misunderstood and said briskly, "Here, here, my girl! You're shivering. Come along and we'll get you warm."

We started toward Government House with my arm in his. I reminded him, "You haven't told me why you swore. Was it simply your charming way of expressing pleasure at my imperfection?"

He laughed. "No. I was thinking that we haven't actually made a marriage between us. Now, this minute, I want to make you my wife. In every sense of the word."

Remnants of that pain I had earlier suffered threatened to close my throat, but only because of the depth of my feelings.

"In every sense," I agreed hoarsely, but it was evident he understood my smile, if nothing else. His hand tightened its warm, hard grip around my waist.

"Today our luck changes. We'll begin a real life together. And give this poor, benighted island the government it deserves. Felipe has brought back valuable information about a truce—sorry, I hadn't intended to mention that. You must forget you heard."

"So I lose my husband to Le Maréchal again," I complained. "I am becoming quite jealous of him." I hesitated, then tried again where I had failed before. "Ian, please—I beg you to believe me. Do not trust Lieutenant Felipe."

"I know, darling. He was annoying you when I looked out a few minutes ago. But that has nothing to do with his skill or his loyalty."

"Ian! In God's name, listen to me!"

I had caught at his arm in my effort to convince him, but he released my fingers easily, throwing me only a crumb of comfort. "We have each other now No more lies the way it was with my first—the way it was before. I'll come to you soon." He smiled, crushed my fingers in his, and let them go.

"I will count the minutes, until you come," I promised, and under the warmth in his eyes I, too, was able to smile. "Darielle and I will go in by the servants' hall. But don't trust anyone. Especially . . . please be careful, Ian."

"Strange, I never liked my name until today. And I promise you, I will be careful. I have a special reason now."

We left him at the portico. He looked happy and confident, but in the midst of our delight in each other, I was haunted by my fears and doubts: it was as if I were seeing him like this for the last time.

Darielle and I were passing through the short transverse hall to the servants' stairs when we heard voices raised. Somewhere nearby, probably in the servants' dining room, Lieutenant Felipe was arguing with a woman. I stopped and listened.

"It was not as you think. It was a joke. I swear it. Only a joke."

Then the woman's voice. Tirsa. She spoke with the commanding tone of one who expected to be obeyed— curious conduct for a freedwoman to use toward an officer of the ruling army.

"You do not make jokes with the life of the governor's woman. Do you hear me, boy? If you touch that woman, even if you fail in your attempt, I will betray you. I swear it!"

Darielle was on a step above me. I motioned her

closer, and whispered, "We must tell the governor. He will have to believe us both."

She stared at me. I hurried her up the stairs, and reaching the floor above, I repeated my plea, this time more forcefully. She looked stupefied with fear.

"Darielle, you heard! You know what Lieutenant Felipe is. We must tell the governor together."

She shook her head, her huge eyes still staring at me. "I cannot, madame. I dare not."

"Are you too one of them?" I asked her sternly.

Again she shook her head, but she would say nothing more. She was not to be trusted, any more than the other servants were, but I could scarcely lay any blame upon a girl like Darielle when she was surrounded every hour by rebel sympathizers. I thrust by her and hurried through the hall to my sitting room. Someone had moved a small three-legged mahogany table into the center of the room, and an elegant, sealed sheet of paper had been propped against a branch of candles. An invitation, no doubt. At least Colonel Douglas's new wife had impressed one of our banquet guests.

I felt too sodden and too worried over Lieutenant Felipe to trouble myself about invitations. In my bedchamber I rubbed my body thoroughly with one of the towels the girls had left in a corner after my bath that morning. I would have to speak to them about cleaning up more promptly. No matter. I must tell my husband this new development with his lieutenant before he came to me expecting the fulfillment we had both desired so passionately. I found a new shift and stockings, a petticoat and gown, and dressed rapidly.

I left my bedchamber so quickly that my overskirt caught upon the table that formed an awkward obstacle in my sitting room. The sealed letter slipped to the floor, and I snatched it up as I hurried out into the hall. My first glance at that precise and beautiful penmanship sent chills of revulsion through me. Revulsion and horror. I knew that precise hand very well. Many a missive had been received by my parents from Luc Monceau, and I myself was the luckless recipient of not a few with Monceau's sinister instructions to attend a ridotto or a small party or an Admiralty ball where he would be "honored" to see me.

In the hall, while I walked on mechanically, I ripped the seal and read the page:

*"Chérie, Now that you are so well situated in the very household of this clod of a governor, nothing could better suit our plans. One day, in Paris, I hope to thank you as the Imperial French Government, and perhaps the Emperor himself, will thank you, but more personally.*

*"I am forced to vacate my rooms in London. A great pity. I had grown so accustomed to them. They were in many ways remarkably useful in our profession. But one must always contend with traitors, and I am afraid we have one in our midst.*

*"A thousand good wishes, my love, until that love is consummated again in the not too distant future, L."*

Dear God! To send a lying, foul letter like this, to have it left on a table where any servant might read it . . . or my husband! I would lose Ian's love, his respect—and my own life! But of course, the thing was deliberate. It had been placed so that someone else would see it. *Had anyone seen it—despite the seal?*

I remembered my dream, and the tight, terrible pain in my throat. Panic threatened to overwhelm me again, but I held myself rigid, and tried to think.

# *15*

Who had left the letter in my room? This was the more important matter. But first, I must get rid of it. I started back to my room, then observed one of the ugly, utilitarian storm lamps that remained lighted all day in the shadowy upper hall. I took the paper to the nearest lamp, removed the globe, and burned the letter to cinders, scorching my fingers in the process.

I felt faint with momentary relief when I had destroyed the last scrap of paper. Shaken by the events of the past few days, I wanted nothing so much as to rest—genuinely to rest—without nightmares, safe and secure in my husband's love and protection.

It was almost dark now. Ian would be readying the search for Le Maréchal. And he was counting upon Lieutenant Felipe's aid. My suspicion had fixed upon Felipe first as the person who had openly left the letter on that table, but as I considered, I had a sudden memory of Tirsa's head at the window of my sitting room, while I was on my preposterous expedition after the devil doll.

I stormed along the hall and down the servants' stairs. I saw Pepine supervising a young man in the setting of the table in the servants' dining room. She glanced my way in the slightly superior manner she often used with me, but I was much more concerned about her own superior, Tirsa. I missed her in the stillroom, where the busy cook's assistant said she had just left. I was not quite certain where Tirsa's quarters were, but when I left the stillroom, returning to the main wing of the house, I nearly collided with her as she stepped into the hall from one of the small salons. As always, she behaved with decorum; she curtseyed, gave me her imperious but oddly sad look, and would have gone on.

"Did you bring anything into my room this afternoon?" I demanded.

"Madame! What thing? I do not understand."

"Was there any mail, perhaps delayed in delivery from the *Maud Vester?*"

"But the *Maud Vester* sailed on the morning tide yesterday. Madame, were you expecting news? But that cannot be. You were aboard the ship!"

"Yet," I said, trying to hold my fury within myself, "other, faster ships have arrived from England. Ships that left British harbors after the *Maud Vester* sailed, have come and gone, have they not?"

She was genuinely puzzled; I felt certain of that.

"If they arrived with mail franked in England, madame, it would have been given to you the hour you arrived at Government House. Is there some mail that you have awaited and which you have not received? I will question the servants at once." Mechanically, she wiped her clean hands on her skirts.

"I want to know who delivered a letter to my room this afternoon, while I was away."

More than ever bewildered, she waved her hands before her as if to free herself of a net of cobwebs. "I cannot say. I do not know. I saw a letter laid against a candlestick. I was not interested. I went to the window. That is all. The letter was there when I left."

"Why did you go into my room, Tirsa?"

"I heard the governor's voice from his study and I—I was curious. I looked out the window."

She might be perfectly sincere about the letter but she was lying now.

"Shall I tell you why you looked out the window?" She backed away from me but seemed unable to make a denial. "You were afraid of what Lieutenant Felipe might do. Isn't it so?"

"But the letter you speak of, madame—no! It was something else entirely."

"Listen to me! I must know. The letter!"

She held herself so stiffly that I realized I must look as though I would use physical violence.

"Believe me, madame, I know nothing of a letter." Then her expression softened. She had seen someone behind me. "It is true. I do not lie, monsieur."

I felt my husband's hands upon my forearms. His grip was hard and painful, but I knew that I had behaved badly, not only shouting like a harridan, but doing so there in the hall with the world as witness. More terrifying, however, was my realization that he had heard me speak of the letter.

Still standing behind me, he moved me away from Tirsa, and drew me into a room two doors away. I had never seen the chambers at this end of the long, ground-floor hall, and was surprised to find myself in a gentleman's bed-sitting room. A clutter of books spilled onto a shelf within arm's reach of a heavy, comfortable-looking milord chair whose cushioned left arm was badly worn. I suspected he must often sit in this chair with his legs draped over the left arm, reading what proved to be innumerable books on the islands of the Caribbean and such oddities as *Experiment in Democracy—A History of the Late North*

*American Colonies,* and *Man's Hope for Utopia—The Western Isles.*

I tried to release myself as gently as possible from Ian's clasp without suggesting that his touch was distasteful to me. Surely he could not know that he hurt me; he did not suspect his own strength. Attempting to free myself so that I might face him, I lightly remarked on his study.

"So this is your haven! And very comfortable it is!" He had more or less propelled me forward, so that I faced the room, and I now saw his bed, large and severe, lacking tester or curtains, but covered simply with sheets, stiff and cool.

My first sight of that bed excited me in a way that I doubted he could guess by his suddenly painful way of pushing me about. But although I wanted and loved him, I found his manner tonight extraordinary, even for him. Had I not known better, I should have guessed he positively disliked me. He must strongly disapprove of my shouting at his housekeeper.

"Ian, it seems I spend all my days apologizing to you, but I am convinced there is a connection between your housekeeper and Lieutenant Felipe. Darielle and I heard her threaten to expose—"

His harsh voice, even more than the words, shocked me.

"We will forget Felipe, damn it! Look at me!" He swung me around to face him. I had a dreadful, despairing suspicion that he knew the contents of Luc Monceau's letter. He looked disheveled, strange in the white shirt without his usual elegant jacket—just the shirt and breeches.

He shook me until I thought my teeth would rattle. "You know what it is, don't you? You hell's spawn! You're white as milk. You must have thought me a great fool, you and your precious spymaster!"

"Ian, listen to me. . . . Let me tell you the truth!"

"When did you ever tell me the truth? You said you had no lover!"

In a daze, as I clutched him to keep from falling, I tried to get in a word in my own defense.

"He lied. He was never my lover. Never!"

"You forget—I knew you had only accepted me because you'd quarreled with your lover. Well, I'd no objection. I need that estate you inherited. I can't do any good in this godforsaken land without a few thousand guineas to spend."

"Please . . ." I whispered, trying to keep his furious taunts straight in my dazed mind. "If you believe . . ."

"Liar!" His eyes were bright and terrible, and still they excited me. If only he could know the truth! Why couldn't he read it in my face, my eyes? "If there is one thing in all this damnable world I hate, it is a liar!"

"I was afraid of him," I managed to explain against his ferocious display of temper. "He wrote that letter to destroy me."

"And had it delivered to my study, not half an hour ago?" he demanded, heavily sarcastic, propelling me across the room.

"Yes! Yes! Why else would he have it placed where you could read it. Why else? If you will only let me prove—"

"I wanted you to prove it. I desired you that first day. But I wanted you to love me, not just to prove something. Now, I will take what I can get."

I broke away from him at the very instant he let me go. I crashed against the bedpost, knocked breathless, and he picked me up like a bundle of straw and threw me onto the bed. I was terrified and sad and in pain all at the same time. I repeated on rising notes of hysteria, "But I do love you! I have from the first day."

"Give me proof!"

Suddenly besieged by his hard, ruthless body, I gasped, found myself weeping, and yet, even in my despair, I understood his fury. I received his attack upon me without revulsion, for I had not lied when I swore that I loved him. During those scorching, frightening minutes of our union, I think he could not have denied that he loved me as well.

But then it was over. He had demonstrated his mastery of his wife, and still he hated me. Now more wretched than he, I watched him later as he left his room. I said nothing: I knew my own defeat. If, in his own bed, I had not convinced him that he was the only man in my life, then he would never believe me. In the doorway he turned, and I knew an instant's hope that vanished as quickly as it had come.

He looked more pale than I had ever seen him, and his face was set, like the judge's in my dream.

"Be gone by the morning, madam! Be out of Government House and gone. If I find you here when I return, by God, I'll have you shipped to London myself where you can stand in the traitor's dock with your French lover!"

Long after he had gone, I relived that bitter condemnation, wondering if I could have said something, anything, to make him believe me. When I heard the men gathering on the drive before setting out on their expedition, with Ian still counting upon the loyalty and aid of Lieutenant Felipe, I went to the window of my husband's room and looked out. I saw that the small company of men would be easily outnumbered by Le Maréchal's rebels. By the lamplight on the portico I could just see Tirsa's silhouette standing in front of one of the pillars.

This was my last chance, perhaps the last time in my life that happiness would be so close, even as it slipped from me. My pride was gone, and my common sense which had told me that nothing I did or said would sway Ian Douglas. He was an explosive man, and there was a flimsy chance that I might still appeal to those violent emotions of his.

I dressed quickly, and flew along the hall to his study. Opening the door, I found him there with several officers, Lieutenant Felipe prominent among them. I had not counted on that. No matter. I squared my shoulders, resolved to rise above the humiliation of my disheveled gown and what surely must be the marks of my husband's unwilling passion upon my face and bare throat.

I made my way between the soldiers, praying that Ian would not repulse me out of hand. The officers' expressions indicated they thought it quite natural that I should appear to wish my husband good fortune in his undertaking. All except Lieutenant Felipe. His heavy-lidded eyes regarded me with a kind of suppressed amusement. I could not begin to imagine what he was thinking. Had he been truly loyal to my husband, I might suppose he was delighted that a traitor, as he probably knew me to be, had been found out.

One of the other men smiled, and made some polite remark which I did not heed. I was moving toward my husband. The others made way. He looked stormy and unforgiving as he saw me, but I walked on. Just before I reached him, I stepped upon a pebble or a clod of dirt brought in on the boot of one of the soldiers. As my ankle turned, Ian reached out instinctively, a twist of concern banishing his scowl.

But Felipe and another officer stepped forward at the same time, and seeing that his support was not needed, Ian jerked his hand back, bowed to me stiffly, and said in a voice that seemed to plunge knives into my last hope, "Good-bye, madam. Good-bye."

He passed me without another glance and was gone, shortly to be followed by his officers, including Lieutenant Felipe.

I stood there stupefied, feeling my world retreat from me. I leaned against his desk until my thoughts cleared. Then I hurried out to the portico in time to see my husband and his officers ride away, followed by the marching men. They would not get far through Le Maréchal's own territory, marching as they were now, but my husband knew these people. I wondered if he had some other plan, and perhaps all this panoply of battle was for mere show, perhaps to mislead the spies serving Le Maréchal. I prayed that this was so.

I turned and trudged across the portico, where I caught Tirsa as she too went back into the house. She started nervously when she saw me, but I let her know at once that I was no longer hysterical. I said quietly, "Tirsa, Darielle and I both heard what you said to Lieutenant Felipe this afternoon." When she opened her mouth, I went on. "How can you send Colonel Douglas out on a jungle campaign with an adjutant who is a traitor?"

"No, madame. That is quite true." The flatness of her voice, the lack of passion, puzzled me.

"But the colonel should have been warned. I tried, but—"

Her next words further astonished me, although the deadness of her dark eyes should have prepared me.

"I have just warned him. He only said 'Allow me to know more of Felipe than my housekeeper does.'" I caught my breath as Tirsa went on. "Madame, Felipe is my son."

There was nothing I could do to help her in her misery. She had found it necessary to betray her own son, and the betrayal had accomplished nothing. Now she really looked at me for the first time.

"You do love the colonel, do you not, madame?" I said nothing and she added, "He has a plan. You need not fear. It is a good plan. I do not know if Felipe is aware of it, but the colonel knows."

I could not tell her that her own son had driven the final wedge between Ian and me, if, indeed, it was Lieutenant Felipe who acted as Luc Monceau's agent and gave my husband a copy of the letter I had found in my room.

"I must leave before the governor returns. I must hurry."

"Madame!" She started after me as I went up the central staircase. "Was it a quarrel? Believe me, madame, Colonel Douglas loses his temper often. It is nothing. He is a good man. He is always sorry after."

In my case he would not be sorry after. In his eyes I would always be a liar, a cheat, a traitor. If I were capable of killing, I thought, I would return to Europe and hunt down Luc Monceau. But I was not a killer. It was only bitterness that filled my thoughts with the blood of revenge.

"It is wrong, madame," Tirsa was saying as she followed me. "You must stay. He will need you if—when he returns."

Booted feet pounded across the portico, and Tirsa

stepped back and went to the reception hall. I heard the murmur of her low voice, then that of my cousin George, loud and confused.

"Well, gad's life, he would have waited for me had he known! I've a deal to tell him. That sailor of Mrs. Mabberly's, the one who died—but it's of no consequence to you, Tirsa, my dear. Which road have they taken?"

I took a long, painful breath. Ian had made it quite clear to me, with that last good-bye, that there was no room for hope. I leaned over the upstairs balustrade and called to my cousin, "George, I must see you."

He came to the foot of the stairs, and peered up at me. "No time, cuz. By the bye, you'd never guess who that chap was. I mean, what he was up to. The dead sailor."

"You mean, the man who tried to kill you and me. I think he was a spy for Le Maréchal."

He looked crestfallen that I knew so much.

"Who the deuce told you? Old Ian, I suppose. Sorry. Can't help you. The colonel needs me more."

I wanted to scream with frustration at him instead. "George! Come here this minute!"

Poor George recognized in that command the echo of our childhood relationship. He galloped up the stairs two at a time, protesting but obedient.

"See here, I've got to get on. The men will need me."

"Did Colonel Douglas order you to join the expedition?"

"No. Officially, I'm off duty. Captain Webb is in Port Fleur. But damn, if I'm needed—!"

Like a driven vessel, I tried a different tack. "I need you more, George. You've gone off duty. And I must ask your advice. Then you may join your men."

He hesitated, then climbed the last steps. "What ails you, cuz? You look ghastly."

"George, my relationship with Ian has ended. I must leave St. Sebastien as soon as possible." His sleepy eyes opened wide, and before he could pour out endless questions, I asked, "What ships are sailing tonight?"

"Tonight? But my dear girl, the tides—no ship out of Port Fleur, until the Dutch brig *Rynsault*. That's two mornings away. If you'd made this discovery yesterday, you might have sailed with that Yankee smuggler." He grinned. "Felipe says she's hove to at Esterby Harbour, probably bringing in rifles and taking out rum. But Felipe missed them. Met the captain's wife, though. Perfect lady, he said, oddly enough."

"George, I've tried in every way—even Tirsa has tried—to warn Ian against Lieutenant Felipe. But he persists in trusting him."

George guffawed. "What? Old Felipe? He's my friend. A rare lad for holding his liquor. . . . Well, cuz, what's it to be?"

While he rambled on about Esterby and the Yankee captain's wife, I began making plans.

"I'll be ready in fifteen—no, ten minutes. I am going to Esterby by the South Coast Road. I intend to sail on that Yankee smuggler."

"You're mad! My dear girl, I've no objection to smugglers. But Yankees!" He trailed along after me to my sitting room, where I stopped him firmly.

"George dear, if you are able to join my husband, please try to protect him. But first, would you see if there is a woman's saddle and a horse I can ride?"

"Heigh-o. Should be. I'll do it for you, cuz. When the French governor was in this house his mistress often rode. By the bye, I'm told our Tirsa used to rule the roost here." Then he loped off.

I tried to be as good as my word, and to ready myself within ten minutes, but I was forced to search for my old portmanteau and was five minutes late when I reached the semi-circular drive, there to find Cousin George with two mounts. He shrugged at my gratitude.

"Same direction. Thought I might start in from Esterby, get the line of where the rebels are hiding, and make my way around the band. Probably be of bigger help this way than following the drum, so to speak."

"Thank you, George." I kissed his cheek and he boosted me up on the skittish mare, attaching the portmanteau behind me on the saddle. He then swung up into the saddle of a stallion very like Ian's. I daresay it was one of Ian's mounts, but it took George's gangling length with reasonable patience, and we were just starting off when Tirsa came running out to us.

Looking up at me, she pleaded, "He loves you, madame. I swear the governor loves you. Whatever has happened between you, you must not regard it."

I closed my hand over hers. "Thank you. You are very generous. But he has ordered me to leave St. Sebastien, and I must go. Good-bye."

I felt that part of her concern was due to her suspicion that Lieutenant Felipe had been in some way responsible for our parting, but I liked her nonetheless for that. Her own suffering must be intense if, as I was now convinced, she felt a genuine loyalty to my husband. But I was reminded suddenly of another painful matter. I removed my wedding ring and put it into her palm.

"Please give it to him, and take care of him for those who love him."

She nodded. George set out, and I joined him seconds later. I wanted to look back but punished myself by refusing to do so until we had nearly reached the South Coast Road. I glanced over my shoulder then, and saw the faint lights flickering on the upper floor of Government House. I wondered if I would carry that last view to my grave.

The stars were out but the moon had not yet risen, and I was painfully reminded of the previous night's horrible events, which began for me along this very road.

"Sad to be leaving old Ian?" my cousin asked. He must have been watching me for some time, anxious over the journey, worried about my own possible decision to return at the last minute.

"Heavens, no! Sad to be leaving Government House perhaps. It was very pleasant, although I think I would have to grow used to the climate."

*But what is my life to be now?* I wondered. *What do I know of the Yankees' huge land? Can I ever be happy there? Or anywhere after what I have done?*

Surprisingly soon, we passed the trail into the region of the Boiling Lake. I glanced that way and then looked quickly ahead. We had turned off here last night, Lieutenant Aaba and I. Was Ian somewhere in that swamp, aimlessly pursuing men who knew that poisonous morass as they knew the veins of their hands?

I hadn't been on horseback—at least, not alone—in many months, and I was soon weary, but I dared not stop or turn back. The muscles in my neck tightened and I began to imagine that I felt the now familiar choking sensation. An attack of nerves, of course. I was afraid for us, traveling at a loud gallop along the now deserted road, but I was more haunted by the thought that I would never see my husband again.

"Some of the French governor's aides and ladies had

little villas here along the coast. Some of them still live there. Up on that cliff to our left. See? And down here just where we come out over the ocean."

I sat forward, peering up into the jungle which grew down close to the road. My knee was nearly paralyzed as it held me erect around the horn of the saddle. If only I could have ridden astride, I should have found myself far more comfortable. While I was trying to catch a glimpse of the little darkened villa, I had to duck my head—one of the night-prowling bats swooped down over us and then up again, into those faintly waving treetops that told us nothing of the millions of hidden eyes, the endless life within.

Devastatingly tired, I found myself falling back. George rode ahead, waited, then rode ahead again. I knew that like all good riders, he hated to be held back. The moon had risen, and I could make out the foam on the rolling surf to my right. The road here split in two, one branch leading to a shelf just above the rocky beach, and the other turning slightly inland, around a huge, tangled clump of roots and ancient trees. I followed George along the inland trail which narrowed perceptibly almost at once. The moon had finally risen, but now became dim little stabs of light seen at great distances. I called to George. He was getting too far ahead. My voice seemed to shimmer through the high fern fronds that enclosed me.

I must have called his name several times before I admitted my fears to myself, and by this time the mare had caught the contagion. Long, entangling vines hindered our passage. I had to reach out, tearing them away time and again. The stalks clung to my glove, like loathsome, hairy things from which I could only free myself with enormous effort. Panicking, the mare blundered, forced me into a thicket, and when I reined in, she suddenly reared up, unseating me. I tumbled into water-soaked brush and huge, vermillion flowers. I was shaken, but not badly hurt. I heard the mare thrashing through the jungle, and I began to call George again.

My own voice, shouting my cousin's name, came back to me eerily through endless corridors in the jungle growth, corridors laced over with vines whose spider-web hairs glistened in the first touches of moonlight. I spun around, starting to call once more, but the hideous echo came back to me like a child's rondeau, bits and pieces repeated. . . .

George! That maddeningly incompetent creature!

I would have to get on to Esterby by myself. I thought I could tell the way, for in my escape from Le Maréchal's men I had touched on the swamp just before reaching Esterby Harbour. So I had best not make my way further into the jungle, even to avoid the swamp. I heard something thrashing about to the east of where I stood on a large clod of mud and grass. That would be the unfortunate mare who had given me a toss.

Furiously banishing the fears that this place inspired, I started to follow the trail of torn shrubbery made by the panicked horse, but the dense vegetation concealed watery depths, as I soon found. I was just pulling my foot back when a hideous noise split the tiny sounds of night. Horrified, I fell against a gigantic tropic bush. A human scream, I thought for an instant—the shriek of someone in agony. But as the awful sounds went on, I knew it was my runaway mare, caught somewhere nearby in swamp waters so deep as to be virtually bottomless. I covered my ears but the hideous noises went on and on.

I turned back, stumbling, repeatedly losing my bal-

ance as I pressed my palms against my ears and tried
to make my way against the dangling, clinging lianas
and unexpected protuberances of mud and rock. But
the vines seemed to have woven new webs in the few
minutes since I had passed through them.

I found myself calling to George again, screaming
his name to drown out the noise of the dying animal.
It seemed darker when I clawed my way back the path
by which I had come. It would have been better to go
on, in spite of what had happened to the mare. At
least there was a trickle of moonlight, not this dreadful dark.

I fell, scrambled up filthy with mud and sodden
leaves, and listened. Except for the sibilant whisper of
water somewhere close by, and the distant flutter of
wings as a night bird took wing, there were no other
sounds. Then, while I was making my way thankfully
over a little island of solid ground, I heard what must
be George's voice in the far distance.

"Madeline, where are you? Call me. Let me hear
you. Where are you?"

That welcome voice brought me out of my stupor
of fear. I answered, "I am here, George. To the west
of you!"

I fought my way through a patch of pale, ghostly
blooms and found the going easier by pursuing
George's voice. I was hopelessly lost in false directions
now, and I followed the path of least resistance. But it
seemed to me, when I heard George's voice calling my
name again, that it came once more from all directions. The wind off the sea groaned through the foliage high over my head and I, catching my foot in
something yielding and soft, screamed, "George, where
are you? Help me!"

He would not come in time . . . I was too tired, too

confused . . . I could hear George coming toward me, splashing through the swampy undergrowth, but as fast as I drew my foot out of the soft mud, I found my other foot sinking in the bottomless, bubbling mass. I had somehow reached the swamp again. Creatures moved around me, churning or slipping by, a few splashing with a loud, froglike croak. I felt my flesh crawl with spidery legs. . . .

I screamed, and at last George was there on firm ground, hardly more than an arm's length away from me. His face looked gray in the slivers of moonlight. He stammered. I had never seen him so terrified.

"T-take care, old girl. The Boiling Lake empties through here s-somewhere."

"Where?" I asked frantically. "Where?"

I reached for him. He seemed to slide from my grasp, as help slips away in a nightmare.

"Madeline, why do you have to make it so hard on yourself? You know we don't leave Luc Monceau. No one ever has. Madeline, it's all your fault. Your fault!"

His voice echoed and re-echoed through the swamp, but its meaning blurred into nonsense. I went on asking for his help several seconds after I knew he was Luc's agent. Then I tried to backtrack, to step precisely where I had been when I slipped off into the swampy runoff of warm mud that embraced my feet like a hideous lover, but this time I could not mistake his intent. He wrenched my hands off the low tree limb I had groped for, and shoved his boot against me. He was more hysterical than I. Nature, it seemed, had not cut him out to be a murderer.

"Oh, God, why don't you die! The devil doll warned you. I did my best to carry out Luc's orders, Madeline. . . . You think I wanted this? I hoped you would die without my raising a hand. They could have done it the other night when they captured you."

"George!"

"I can't help it. Don't you see? Not my fault. If you don't die this time, Luc will have me killed. That sailor from the ship—he gave me the letters, told me I had to pay you off for your betrayal, or Luc would send others after me. And he will! You know it, Madeline!"

"George—" I tried to be very calm, not to move. "—Luc can't hurt you now. He has been betrayed in London, but not by me. He has fled London. He has no power now, except through his agents, people like you."

George's long face looked haggard, wretched in the moonlight. "You always gave me orders. Even as a child, Madeline. But not after I joined Luc Monceau. Your father helped me into the band. He said no Adare would ever serve the English."

The sins of the father, I thought. My own father had brought George and me to this pass.

"Luc made me—don't you see? Made me go into the army. Bore from within, he said. I can't let you live now—don't you see?"

"And you used those lying letters of his to destroy me! I was never his mistress. I loathed him!"

He cried frantically, "Only at the last I used them. When everything else failed. I was ashamed of that. It was dishonorable about the letters."

But everything else, including my murder, was less dishonorable? Well, perhaps in his poor mind that was so. He had followed orders all his life. If not mine, then some other taskmaster's. My father's. And Luc Monceau's. I had always known I could handle him. George had been so easy, so cheerful and obliging. Always afraid of a sharp word, of disapproval, of not doing as he had been bidden.

I must save myself. I had always relied upon myself. I tried again to step precisely where I had stepped a few minutes before. I succeeded. One more step and I should be upon solid ground. Fern fronds rustled against my arms, my face. I shuddered. A swamp creature slithered past me.

"There!" George cried, quite beside himself. "One of those snakes will do the thing. Not my fault!"

But when I tried to pull myself free of the rushes and ferns, he reached out again with one muddy boot, crashing it into my thigh, such a breathtaking jolt as I had never felt before. The pain stabbed through me. I heard the echo of my moaning, my own breathless efforts at survival while I stumbled on the brink of the boiling mass beneath.

"Madeline," he begged, piercing the sound of my struggles, "make it easier for me. You always did the hard things. Always helped me. Die! If you don't, Luc will send someone to kill me. Madeline, please . . ."

Then the swamp exploded with lights, so many that they blinded me. But when I closed my eyes the nightmare lost itself in the one dream that had ever stirred me: I was picked up and lifted high into a man's arms. I knew and loved that man. But Ian was far from this place, I knew that. So it must be a fantasy, and in my death struggle my mind had summoned up the one great happiness of my life.

# 16

The sunlight was so bright against my closed eyelids that I could only peer out beneath my lashes. To my astonishment I made out a broad black face with wise eyes framed by small square spectacles.

"Ah!" his deep voice remarked with satisfaction. "Coming around, I see. Your excellency need concern yourself no longer. The poultice on the thigh and a good rest was all your lady required."

"How very odd!" I murmured.

"How so, madame?" the kind man prompted me.

"If I am dead, I should be in hell. But it isn't nearly hot enough." I watched through my lashes, hoping this serious statement would provoke a laugh from "his excellency" who must surely be my husband. I felt that I could not turn my head without giving myself a blinding headache, and only his laugh would assure me of his presence. Then he did better than laugh. Ian came forward to the bedside, and in an unexpectedly shaken voice, said, "Thank you, Doctor. You have been most helpful. I am grateful to your—to Le Maréchal for sending you with us."

The surgeon got up, making room at the bedside for my husband, who looked as though he had spent a night without sleep. There was a bruised and swollen lump over his left temple which, for some obscure reason, made him more attractive to me. But his dark eyes looked so anxious that it was hard to believe he was the same evil-tempered man who had assaulted me only hours before.

"And in this very bed!" I cried in surprise as I opened my eyes and looked around, for we were certainly in his bed-sitting room on the ground floor.

He grinned at that, and I heard the door close as the surgeon left us alone. He bent over my face and kissed me, softly and gently.

"No, this cannot be my husband," I murmured sadly. "I wonder what stranger it may be." He studied me, his eyes narrowing, and I went on, "How terrible to have my love turn into a gentleman!"

He laughed aloud then, loud enough for the surgeon to open the door, peer in anxiously, then with a nod of satisfaction, close the door again.

"Damned if that bastardly cousin of yours, with his sly tricks, didn't have me thinking the worst of you. My darling, why didn't you tell me about that frippery French rascal you were so terrified of?"

"Not frippery, I am afraid, sir. Luc Monceau was the master of French agents in England. He had an agent on the *Maud Vester*—that sailor—with orders to frighten George into doing his duty against me. They may have tried to rid themselves of me on shipboard, but I was sick half the time and in my cabin. And then, too, I don't think either of them had the courage."

Ian shook his head as he took one of my hands. Then he brought it to his lips with all the gallantry of a Carlton House beau.

"I don't believe he had the nerve. I always suspected Adare would show the white feather. But he was obliging. Did as he was told. Curious how likable we all

found him. Made himself indispensable, I daresay.
. . . I nearly broke his back there in the swamp."

"How in heaven's name did you find us?"

"You were hardly silent, my love. We heard you
calling. After Felipe brought Le Maréchal and me together, it was Le Maréchal who told me he had seen
Adare leading my wife toward the Boiling Lake. But
Felipe himself was walking a thin line. He had a loyalty both to Le Maréchal and to me."

"Wait!" I begged him. "Begin again. My poor head!
You mean that Lieutenant Felipe was trying to bring
you and Le Maréchal together? I thought he was loyal
to the rebels." No matter what Ian believed, I would
never entirely trust the serpentlike Felipe, but I did
him the justice of thinking that he might be loyal to
Ian without liking me!

"And he was loyal to the rebels. But he told me all
his movements. Le Maréchal is his father."

"My God!" I fell back on the pillows. "Then Tirsa
is Le Maréchal's wife."

Ian contradicted me with a rueful grin. "Well, not
precisely. They both began life as slaves. But they
went their different ways. There were few enough
marriages among them in those days, even after they
were freed. Then Tirsa became the mistress of the
French governor, and there was precious little commu-
nication between Tirsa and Le Maréchal, I suppose. I
don't know how all this will end, but the rebels and I
will be meeting again today, and for however long it
takes, until we find a peaceful solution. I owe Le
Maréchal your life. That should count for something.
If I hadn't met him there last night we should not
have discovered you and your delightful cousin until
too late."

"And you marched all those men off last night to no

purpose at all! You intended all the time to meet the rebel chief in private."

He was remarkably cheerful over it. "On the contrary. They benefited by the exercise. And their real mission was to intercept a cargo of rifles being smuggled to the rebels. Felipe and I left them to beat the jungle while we rode off to meet Le Maréchal and a couple of his lieutenants in the swamp, near Esterby. It was Le Maréchal who told us of Adare's attempts to sew discord."

I was sickened by a sudden thought. "But you still believed that letter told the truth about me! You hadn't forgiven me even when you saved my life."

"I am happy to say your cousin convicted himself on that score. We all heard him threatening you, pleading with you to die and save him some little trouble in the matter. Le Maréchal and I both heard him admit that the letters were that fellow Monceau's method of destroying you if his homicidal sailor failed. At all events, I was so frantic that I ran directly into one of those damned trees with a dozen trunks, and hence the battered countenance. Otherwise, I should have reached you a minute earlier. But we have Adare's full confession and his signature."

I sighed, "Poor George. My father brought him into that vile business, he says. I feel responsible somehow . . . Ian, what will happen to him?"

"He certainly cannot return to Britain or Ireland. Or any place where the Army or Navy is stationed." I nodded. He had a peculiar smile, very odd in the circumstances. "I hope you will agree we had to put him somewhere out of mischief." I nodded again, more slowly, wondering what was to come. "There happened to be a Yankee vessel in the harbor at Esterby, a brig trying to supply the rebels with guns. Having failed in this, they lost three seamen in a scuffle with my men. We obligingly gave them your cousin George and sent them on their way with our blessing."

"Good Lord! That kind of work will kill poor George. He has never had to do any manual labor."

"I doubt it will kill him," Ian said drily. "I confess I feel sorry for the Yankees who inherit him, but I dare say they will be warned by the brig's captain who knows the story. As far as George is concerned, it is certainly more pleasant than hanging in London."

I did not remind him that he had threatened me with that same death, but he must have thought of it.

He leaned close to me again. Although his voice was faintly husky with emotion, his eyes held that brightness that I remembered from another occasion.

"You talk of my forgiving you. The important thing, my love, is whether you forgive me." He touched the bed beside my body. "I am talking about what happened here."

I looked as innocent as was possible for me to.

"Why do you think I love you?" I said.

He took my face between his hands. For all his apology and talk of forgiveness, his mouth felt hard and strong and passionate upon mine. This time I left him in no doubt that he had met his match.